the
GOOD BOOK
club

RICK DEWHURST

quotidian

Quotidian Books
Duncan, BC

Published by Quotidian Books
Duncan, BC
Printed in Charleston, SC

ISBN: 098674574X
ISBN-13: 9780986745744
LCCN: 2010919317

For Katherine, Rachel, and Matthew

CHAPTER ONE

I only wanted a trim, the split ends snipped a bit, but the kid with the scissors had her own ideas. My number-one miracle worker had gotten herself married; she was on the honeymoon now. That was all that Gilda, a kid with dreams, a new job, and enthusiasm to match, could bubble about when I asked her to go easy on my delicate self-image. I wasn't in the mood for her naive joy this morning. And to add to the thrill, the monolith in the next chair was having her hair frozen in time, the smell of the finishing spray mixing with the fishy stink of a recent perm and reminding me of how hard it was to be a lady. Gilda finished the demolition, her *Vogue* cover fantasies intact. The only thing left to do was pay. On my way out, I snickered at the Saucy Kitten sign hanging above the sidewalk below the awning. The name was a bad choice for a dump specializing in hair design. Everyone knew that cats, young or old, coiffed themselves.

Back in the office, I sorted out my Monday, the usual e-mail, spam, bills, junk mail, and stray thoughts of who I'd be dancing with when the party ended. I was between secretaries. I was just as happy. The last one refused to engage my filing system and wanted some respect. I didn't have any to give her. On my descent down the slow road to depression, my cell phone signaled me to take a detour, ringing "What's Love Got To Do With It."

"Sunday Detective Agency," I said.

"Hi, Jane, it's Norman, Norman Parks."

"Hello, Norman. This is a surprise. How are you this morning?"

"I'm good, yes, I would say I'm good. Everything's good with me."

"Good," I said. "I'm good, too."

I was relieved to hear we were both good, even though he sounded too good to be true.

"So, is this a professional call," I said, "or are you raising money for something?"

"It's professional. I'm wondering if you have time to meet me today. I need you to look into a small matter."

I didn't like the sound of that. From experience I knew that looking into things got ugly fast, whether they were small things or not. I had a hunch that dear Norm, son-in-law to the senior pastor of the biggest congregation in Vancouver, hadn't called me to join him for a Bible study.

He said, "Let's say in about an hour. Would Starbucks at Cambie and Tenth be okay, around eleven thirty?"

"It's short notice, but I think I can make it. Are you sure you need my services?"

"Yes, I've heard you're an expert in this kind of thing."

I wondered what range of activity was included in Norm's definition of *this kind of thing*.

"Don't believe everything you hear in church," I said.

"I'll see you then."

"I'm looking forward to it. You can tell me how much you love my new hairdo."

"Right."

He wasn't amused. Something was up, and it didn't sound too heavenly. There were at least a half dozen reasons why a guy like Norm might want to talk to a gal like me, none of them uplifting. But I'd stopped whining about my career choice long ago.

I finished up the morning's drudgery, straightened up the face under the hair, and made my way down to the parking garage. I beeped open my Sunset Orange Hummer, fired it up, and then, braving the September drizzle, bullied the traffic on my way down to Starbucks.

Norm was already hunched over a mocha when I arrived and didn't get up when he saw me coming. It looked like I would be buying my own. I fetched my black grande and went to join him at the table, where he fudged an attempt to rise in my honor. Norm was lean, his short, straight black hair parted on the side, his mustache trimmed like he'd never heard of Adolf Hitler. His black suit jacket failed in its attempt to look comfortable slumming with his jeans. He held his cup with both hands, his excuse for not shaking one of mine. He faked a smile for me and then, looking around the room, faked one for everyone else. As usual, I tried to like him.

"Thanks for coming, Jane," he said.

Norm lifted his cup, dropped his smile into it, and then looked up again to nod at me, like we had an understanding. We didn't.

"I do my best to come when I'm called, Norman. That's what I get paid for."

Norm wriggled in his chair and pulled another grin onto his face, his thin lips disappearing under his black caterpillar. Men like Norm were a dime a dozen. He was a pastor-in-waiting. He'd elbowed his way to the front of the line to wait for the day when his father-in-law, Senior Pastor Jessop, decided it was time to vacate the pulpit. The elbowing action had resulted in a jerky ride for Jessop's prim daughter, Sally, who was forced to clutch Norm's arm with both hands, having agreed to his hasty marriage proposal five years before. No more playing second pulpit for Norm. The opening at the top of his stairway to heaven brightened every day as he ascended to view his future life in his own perfect light. I hoped Senior Pastor Jessop stayed around a while.

"I haven't seen you in church lately," Norm said, taking the high ground.

I wasn't in the mood for dodgeball. Associate Pastor Norm liked to have his official position in the church stroked, but today my nails weren't in a retractable mood.

"It's been a busy month."

I flicked at a piece of fuzz on the arm of my chair. It was attached. The furniture needed refurbishing, a sign of the times.

I said, "Did you ask me here to investigate my apostasy, or did you have something more important in mind?"

Pastor Norm pretended not to ogle a passing young blonde's flesh and bones.

He refocused on me and said, "How did a woman like you get into this kind of business anyway?"

"You sound like you're trying to reform a hooker."

"No, sorry, you know what I mean. You don't seem like the PI type."

"You mean I'm not a man?"

"Okay, yes, that's what I mean, and I understand you're on your own too."

His pastoral compassion for me, a rebellious woman, tugged on my pity for the male of the species, but I refused to fall for it.

"I grew up in the business, and when my father died, he left it to me."

"He's gone then? I'm sorry."

"I'm not. Dear old Dad wasn't kind, but he came by it honestly. His father was no prince either."

"Where was your mother?"

"She had to go before her time. She couldn't live anymore."

"I'm sorry…I…"

"I'd rather not explore my inner child right now. Are you interviewing me for an upcoming inner-healing course at the church, or have you got some use for a private investigator?"

Norm swallowed, and then he gulped a mouthful of mocha, forcing him to swallow again.

"I'll get to the point," he said. "Since you're one of us, I mean, part of the church family, so to speak, I thought you would be the perfect choice to look into a concern I've had for a few months now. But, you see, I don't know exactly how to say it."

"Why don't you just spit it out? I'm over twenty-one."

"Yes, well, I'd like to put it as delicately as I can. You see, my father-in-law has been acting suspiciously. As you no doubt are aware, his wife died last year, a horrible accident, and I'm sorry to say I think he has been seeing a member of the congregation, in a way that is inappropriate to his calling. I'm not positive, but…"

"You mean you want me to find out if our senior pastor is fornicating?"

"If we want to be crude about it, yes, that's one way of putting it, but technically, it would be adultery, since this particular woman I'm referring to is married. You can see how delicate this is and why I'm talking to you about it."

"Shouldn't you be talking to God and your father-in-law about it instead?"

"Yes, of course, that goes without saying. I have talked to him about it, but he's not forthcoming."

I wondered who wasn't forthcoming, God or his father-in-law.

He said, "I'm talking to you because I want to protect him, and if there is moral failure, and I suspect there is, I need to keep it all under wraps, if you see what I mean."

I saw what he meant. I'd heard spiels like his before. Keep it hush-hush for the good of all. He planned to grab the shepherd's staff and prod his father-in-law out to pasture, all the while making it look like he was guarding the flock. He was betting on me to get the evidence he needed and keep it all in the family. No media sticking their noses in and upsetting the parishioners. The church status quo had to be maintained, and I suspected that he was planning to end up with all the status and probably most of the quo, too.

I said, "I might be a little slack getting out of bed on Sunday mornings, but catching my pastor in the act ranks pretty low on my scale of preferred activity."

Norm flinched and shook his head, erasing the image from his mind. I wasn't so lucky.

"I'm not suggesting anything as graphic as that. I only need enough evidence to show him I know what's going on, and then he can do the honorable thing. That way, my wife is saved the embarrassment too. And that way everyone's better off. You'll be doing us all a service."

I wasn't sure this was the way I wanted to contribute to church life. Teaching Sunday School was even more preferable.

"I'd like to talk to your wife before I decide. I'm assuming she does know about it?"

"Yes, of course, and I'm sure Sal will be happy to talk to you. She only wants what's best for her dad and the church."

I was happy to know that he and his gal Sal wanted the best for everyone. Wasn't that what church community was all about?

"I'll call her," I said.

Norm knocked back the last of his mocha. His mustache clogged from the flow. He took his napkin, dabbed at the drippings, and pretended not to observe the rear view of the blonde flesh and bones now exiting.

"You're an attractive woman," he said, his eyes still wayward. "And I understand you're single?"

"Yes, I'm single. Mr. Right never came along."

"That's too bad, I…"

"Let me fill in the picture for you. I'm fortyish, not married, and I've got no prospects. Is there anything wrong with that?"

"No, there's nothing wrong with that. Of course there isn't. Those who have chosen the single life are valuable members of the church."

"Who says I chose it?"

"Well, then, if that's the case, there's still hope. There are a lot of single men out there who would be blessed to find someone as intelligent and attractive as you."

"You're making me blush. But like I said, I'll give Sally a call."

Norm surmised our little talk was over. He stood and smiled at me.

"Let me know what you decide," he said, and then he smiled his way out of the coffee shop, the loving pastor, another good deed done for the day.

I sipped what was left of my black brew and tried not to be bitter.

Back outside I climbed into my Hummer and took a ride down Granville Street. The drizzle had ended, and the September sun, reprising July's good times, steamed the pavement. Getting the scoop on Pastor Jessop, if there was any dirt to dig up, was easy, but did I want the job? Goody Two-Shoes, who'd surfaced in my head, was giving me an argument. I thought she'd gone missing long ago and been forgotten, filed for efficiency's sake under nursery tales and other useless distractions for children. This was just a job, I countered. What difference did it make? A corporate executive, a small-time philanderer, a pastor, the job was the same. Goody Two-Shoes lost. I decided to follow through. Besides, I'd already told Norm I'd talk to Sally, so that's what I would do. Integrity was essential, even if there weren't many who played that way these days. I punched in the numbers, and after two rings she answered.

"Hello?"

"Is that Sally?" I said.

"Yes, hi, and you're Jane, aren't you? Norman said you were going to call."

Although I'd seen her on Sundays gracing the front pew, I'd never heard her voice before, and I wasn't fond of it. It had that familiar black-and-white-and-shallow-all-over lilt that made me queasy. The sound gushed from people who'd grown up in the church, who'd never questioned their world, or walked on the wild side, or even stepped on a sidewalk crack. They were dangerous.

"I was wondering if I might drop around for a heart-to-heart?"

"Yes, of course, any time would do."

"Would in half an hour do?"

"Why, of course, I do know how important this is, so I will make time this afternoon."

"In about half an hour then?"

"Do you know where we live?"

"I've known where you live for a long time."

"You have? That's surprising, but then you're the detective, aren't you? A half hour will be fine. See you then."

I could hardly wait.

Traffic was thick downtown, where make-believe continued to thrive. Our defiant metal, plastic, and rubber machines played jerky follow-the-leader down Georgia Street and through Stanley Park. The sun was still out. The view from Lion's Gate Bridge I took for granted and pointed my nose toward the North Shore, where Norm and Sally had set up housekeeping in their million-dollar abode. Church business had been good to them.

The house was set among a half acre of trees in the British Properties on the side of Hollyburn Mountain. Vancouver sparkled below, its underbelly hidden beneath its stunning tourist costume. Sally met me at the door of their contemporary mountain shack and showed me into the living room. The exposed wood beams and cathedral ceiling lifted my eyes, and the natural light from the large windows on two sides of the room splashed onto their decorator's heavy preference for white. The room's aura captured me, like a raven lost in a luminous cloud. I listened for a choir, but it failed to show. The stone fireplace didn't seem to care. Outside the azure pool gurgled for no one, a hint of chlorine sneaking inside to blend with the vanilla air freshener. I sat in a white leather armchair and tried not to notice.

"Nice house," I said.

"Thank you, we like it. Can I get you something?"

A Cuba libre would have been nice, but I was past all that.

"I could use a cup of tea if you're having one," I said.

"What a coincidence, I just made a pot. It's in the kitchen."

Happy Sally went forth to fetch the tea. She wasn't that plain up close. Her short, dark brown hair was serviceable, and she was plump in the right parts. Her pretty pink dress was just the thing for an afternoon around the house. It looked like it had been starched. A capricious twitch in her gene pool and she might have turned out beautiful. Even the way she was, Norm had done well for himself.

She returned with the pot and the cups on a tray and set it on the glass-and-brass coffee table. She poured it like a spill would cast doubt on her salvation. I took mine straight.

"I won't lie to you," she said, getting right to the point. "My father has been having his challenges lately."

I wondered if she lied to others, and how often, and would she lie to me in the future? But I admired her perspective on adultery.

"So you don't think he's been engaging in extra-Biblical activities?"

"I didn't say that. He's been under a lot of pressure. He's sixty now, and the stress of the job has been enormous over the years, and with Mother gone, I'm afraid he needed an outlet. You see…I don't blame him."

She dug her nails into the palms of her hands and then examined her cuticles.

She didn't blame him. I hoped someone like her was in charge of eternal rewards. I'd blamed my father, and he'd gone to his reward, but punishing hers wasn't my job. I had to keep my thoughts on fatherhood in check.

"Who's the lucky gal?" I said.

"Yes, I am. I have a lot to be…what? Pardon me?"

"Sorry, bad manners are one of the hazards of the business."

Sally reflected in her teacup.

"I understand," she said. "You must have a difficult life."

"It's a living."

"Her name is June Forsythe. She is his secretary. Dad has known her for years."

"And what makes you suspect there's something going on?"

"They've been seen together in different places, talking intimately. You always know when there's more going on than just conversation, don't you?"

I had to agree that I usually did, but I didn't think that was any of her business.

"You say they've known each other a long time. What makes you think they aren't just talking like old friends?"

"Norman has seen her car at his house, in the middle of the day, with no one else around."

"He's been spying on them?"

"It's not spying when there's so much at stake. Dad hasn't been himself. He's getting paranoid too. He thinks there are people in the church who are trying to get rid of him, and to make matters worse, he doesn't want to pastor anymore either. But at the same time, there are people who count on him, and they're afraid that if he leaves, the church will fall apart. He doesn't want to let them down, so he stays."

"What's your opinion?"

"Dad has had enough, and Norman is extremely competent. If there is anyone who would be able to fill Dad's shoes, it would be Norman."

An unsavory thought surfaced to suggest what he might fill his father-in-law's shoes with. I sanitized my mind by drowning the image in the blue of the pool.

"Do you do much swimming?" I said.

"We do, yes, mostly in the summer months."

"I understand you don't have any children?"

"No, we don't, Norman...he...you see...we're not sure if we ever will."

So Norman was destined to come up short on the begats. That was too bad. No wonder he was pushing so hard to get to the top.

"We have thought of adopting, but still, we haven't lost hope," she said.

"I was sorry to hear about your mother. It must have been a terrible loss. How have you been coping?"

"I'm doing fairly well now, I think. Thank you for asking."

Sally looked into her teacup for answers and then got lost there, replaying the day of the accident.

"It was sudden," she said. "Mother was only about a mile from home when it happened. The other driver was drunk, and that was it. She died instantly. That, at least, was a blessing."

I tipped back the dregs of my tea. Sally wasn't so bad. She'd lived her whole life in the church and survived; there was something to be said for that.

Calling her back from her memories, I said, "I'll see what I can find out about your dad and Mrs. Forsythe. And I'll let Norman know I have agreed to take the case."

"Thank you, Jane, and if it is at all possible, please keep my dad from being exposed and humiliated. I would hate for him to finish his ministry this way. He has given a lot over the years. It wouldn't be fair."

I didn't understand how *fair* entered the adultery equation, but Sally seemed to grasp the concept, her illusions intact. She showed me to the door. I was happy to be out of the light. On my way back down the mountain, I called Norm. I told him I wasn't going to charge him for a job like this, and he seemed to know that already. But he agreed to pay my expenses. Crawling over the Lion's Gate in the thick traffic, my orange Hummer blended with the afternoon sun. I noticed the dark clouds blowing in from the southwest. Sooner or later, the fall would have its way.

* * *

CHAPTER TWO

I went straight home. The office would still be there in the morning. My False Creek town house was waiting for me as usual. I unlocked the door to the simple life, my visit with Sally lingering in my mind. She lived in a sterile environment with a husband to match. Who was I to judge? I looked around at my empty nest. Everything was in order. Living alone held few surprises. But for better or worse, there was no man to clutter up my life. I threw my things in the closet and slumped on the couch. Romance was a fool's game, and I wasn't coming out to play. Look what Sally had ended up with. Besides, I didn't want to let Norm down. He placed a high value on me as a single, eligible spinster, seasoned bait for stray middle-aged men who would be lured into his future congregation to be caught and cleaned. But bless him for noticing I was attractive and intelligent, even though he lacked the discernment to see I was brilliant, and humble, the complete blessing for the right man. But there weren't any right men. I knew that. It was demon hope that kept romance alive. And hope never died. Maybe there was a miracle out there for me. But if God was the head matchmaker, he must have misplaced my file. Before my self-pity started to pool, my cell sang. I recognized the name on the display. She was someone I'd been waiting to talk to.

"Sunday," I said.

"Hi, this is Amy, Amy Jessop. Have I caught you at a bad time?"

I wanted to tell her she'd delayed my head from going into the oven, but I didn't want to get off on the wrong foot. I settled for sarcasm.

"Oh, no, I don't have a private life, so now is as good a time as any."

"I'm sorry, I have caught you at a bad time. I'll call you tomorrow, then?"

"No, now's fine," I said. "I wanted to talk to you too. You heard I was up to see your sister?"

"Yes, we're a close family. I called because there are a few things that might be beneficial for you to know before you begin to do whatever it is you people do…do your job, I mean."

Well wasn't this nice; we were going to quarrel. That suited me. The sisters-in-the-faith routine soon wore thin anyway. Then I realized I was the one who started it. I relaxed my upper lip, cloaking my fangs.

"I'd like to hear your *few things*," I said. "The more I know the better."

"I see, well, Ms. Sunday…"

"Never mind the *Ms.*, it's Jane."

"Okay, Jane. Let me…"

"Not over the phone. When would you like to meet to talk this over?"

"This is urgent, or I would have waited until tomorrow. Can you make time this evening?"

"I'll need to cancel my date with *The Bachelor*, but I'm okay with that. I know it would have never worked out. Where would you like to meet?"

"Do you know Digby's on Fourth?"

"A sports bar? Is that the best place for a pastor's daughter to hang out?"

"You're not my mother, and for your information, I ripped that inferior label off when I left home. I'm on my own now."

"Forgive me for my ignorance."

I needed time to shower, wash my hair, and microwave whatever.

I said, "How about eight o'clock?"

"I'll see you then, and thank you."

I felt wanted, three of them in the same family in the same day. Amy was the blonde one, the cute one, and she'd been to college too. She never sat with the rest of them when she came. She sat in the back pew, a loner, no guilt by association. The young, single guys congregated around her, and some not so single.

The trip down Fourth Avenue was stop and go in the thin sheets that passed for an autumn shower. Like the rest of us living here in the West Coast rain forest, I spent a lot of time driving with the wipers on and the windows rolled up tight. But the wet weather here hadn't discouraged the retirement exodus from the colder parts of the country. This was Canada's version of the land of milk and honey, and the local chamber of commerce liked it that way. Toronto was long gone in my mind, and I refused to welcome it back, not even disguised as nostalgia. There was nothing for me to go back for. I was going forward. And now I was going to hear Amy's story as she saw it. From what I'd learned about ministry life, her experience as a pastor's daughter, if she'd been paying attention, would have given her a stirring history to tell.

Digby's was typical jock-and-beer land, and when the Canucks were playing hockey, worship was on. Amy had snagged a table near the end of the bar. Three guys on stools were dividing their devotion between the game and the blonde girl. I thought I was coming to her rescue, but then the coy smile on her face let me know that stirring up the boys was nothing new to her. She added a new dimension to the expression *a babe in Christ*.

"Thanks again for coming," she said.

I pulled up a chair and sat. She was cute, but was that enough? The three guys, puzzled by my arrival, downsized their grins and raised their eyebrows at one another. I tried not to care if they thought I was her mother.

"I don't get out much, so this is a real treat," I said.

"Do you have to do that?" she said.

I was pleased to hear that Amy was sensitive.

"No, but it keeps me from telling the truth," I said.

"I don't mind the truth, so don't spare me."

And she had a functioning brain. That was encouraging. The girl with the tray stooped by, flourishing the goods, and asked me what I wanted.

"I'll have a ginger ale on the rocks. And how about you?" I said to Amy.

She swirled the dregs and nodded.

"Another Bloody Caesar," the efficient girl said and went to fetch them.

"Are those good for you?" I said.

"You really do think you're my mother, don't you?" Amy produced a cheeky smile. She was going to be a handful. Instead of shallow and easy to fathom, she had more depth than the average kid I waded into. I looked forward to enjoying the surprises that might lurk down there. So straight ahead seemed like the way to go.

"What's it all about, Amy? The pastor's naughty daughter routine, I mean?"

She faked sweet circumspection.

"You're right, I haven't always been like this," she said.

"Let me guess, you're twenty-four and bored with life, you haven't found a man yet who's either strong enough or kind enough to put up with you, and you're not that sure God is all they say He is either. Other than that, what else is eating you?"

"You seem to know all about it. Why don't you fill in the rest for both of us, making adjustments for age?"

Our speedy server swooped in to deliver the drinks and interrupt our match. Amy took a satisfied sip of her Bloody Caesar. I decided to let her win the round.

"I presume you called me to talk about your dad," I said.

"They're trying to kill him," she said. Cute, sweet Amy turned ugly sour. Her blonde hair still looked nice.

"Who's they?"

"Norman, of course, and Sister Sally, only Sally doesn't know what she's doing."

"And how are they planning to kill him?" I said.

"With gossip and slander, mostly."

"That's not usually fatal."

"You don't understand. Dad is under too much stress, and he's losing it. He's disintegrating before our eyes. It's cumulative. He's been burnt-out for years, but he keeps on going. God only knows for what reason. In the meantime, Norman and Sally have decided to help finish him off. Sally thinks she's doing it for Dad, so he won't be involved in a sex scandal, that it's best for him to retire, and, of course, that it's for the good of the church. But as for Norman's motives, Norman only wants what's best for Norman. He married Sally because…Oh never mind, there's no point in going there. It hasn't been easy for her."

Amy paused for another sip of Caesar. The boys at the bar were leaning our way.

"Have they told you why they hired me?" I said.

"Of course. Sally told me. That's why I wanted to talk to you before this whole thing about June gets too far. Dad's not having an affair. He and June have been friends for years. Dad might be in poor shape, but he's not desperate. And he doesn't know that Norman is plotting to expose his adulterous affair with June, which of course he's not having, but he suspects that Norman is up to something. He knows Norman is dying for him to retire so he can take his place. And it hurts him. He has tried his best with Norman. He's given his whole life to the church, and now his son-in-law is sticking the knife in. It's a wonder Dad is still sane."

From what I'd seen of Norm, Amy had him summed up pretty well. And if her facts and instincts were right about the alleged affair, I'd been hired to investigate a nonevent. And there wasn't much I could do to protect Jessop from Norm's attempt to usurp the pulpit either. If I wasn't willing to fulfill my role, he'd just hire someone else, or concoct some other way to make his dreams come true.

I said, "Are you sure about your dad and the other woman? That they're not getting cozy on company time?"

"Of course I'm sure. Norman is setting you up to be a pawn in his game. Once you start sticking your nose in things, there will be rumors and innuendos circulating through the congregation that the PI parishioner is investigating the senior pastor for who knows what, and the Lord only knows why. The grapevine gossip will spread until Dad, for the good of the church, will have to step down and into his graceful retirement. It makes you sick, doesn't it?"

"But don't you think it would be better to get the truth out in the open now? Why doesn't your dad confront Norman? Isn't telling the truth the best way to go?"

"That's not how church works. In the first place, Dad doesn't know the details of Norman's plot yet. And if he did, he wouldn't do much about it anyway. If he confronts Norman, the word will get around that there is a rift, and Norman will only think up some other way of achieving his goal. And, besides, Dad is not going to expose Sally and his son-in-law, even if it is Norman. Dad also knows that a confrontation would be a recipe for a church split, and he's not going to allow that. He's doing his best to leave the church healthy when he finally does retire. But Norman only wants to have things his way, and he knows that Dad's not happy with him for a few other reasons, which we don't need to go into. So Norm isn't just going to sit around and risk losing his chance of leading a congregation of eight thousand souls. There are ten other associate pastors on staff, not counting the youth and children's pastors. He's probably afraid that Dad might pass the pulpit to someone else. There's a lot at stake for Norman, and for everybody else in the church, whether they know it or not."

"And Sally, what about her? Where does she really stand in all this?"

"You've seen her, haven't you? She's always been like that."

"There's something to be said for make-believe."

"You mean you saw her collection of romance novels?"

"No, I guessed."

"I think they help keep her sane. Reality's not so great for her."

"I can sympathize. The whole world's a psych ward."

"I guess you would know."

"Yes, I do know. I've had a lot of experience. My dear father showed me the truth about people. I've never forgiven him for it."

The designated pickup man slid our way. He was the slick one with the barbell-inspired body, just a vehicle for a ride into a vacant heaven. But who was I to judge? Amy met his advance with her firm, pretty chin before he could speak.

"Thanks for dropping by," she said, "but my mother needs to get to bed early tonight."

Before he could open his mouth for the obvious come-back, I froze him with my bared fangs. He turned and rejoined his buddies, issuing them a not-worth-the-trouble grunt, and back onto the big screen they focused their lives.

"So, what are you going to do?" Amy said.

"Like my dad used to say, I need to sleep on it."

"I thought you said he wasn't a favorite of yours, and so now you're quoting him?"

"I sugarcoat memories sometimes to make believe our lives were normal. They're easier to swallow that way."

"I'll try to remember that, Mother."

* * *

CHAPTER THREE

I'd said yes to the book club in an empty moment, before the thought of rubbing insights with four other church women could arrive to give my head a shake. And the time, Tuesdays at 7:00 a.m., should have sped an image of the potential chaos front and center, but it was blocked by the notion that intentional sacrifice was required for the sake of community. *The Great Gatsby* was this month's pick. As for me, I'd had enough of the American Dream.

The soft black leather chairs in the coffee shop compensated for the drivel that was bound to ensue, but it was kind drivel, and the gals were well-meaning, and we were learning to cherish the lie that everyone's opinion counted for something. My drivel was as good as anyone else's, and I was growing, being transformed from the caustic outsider to a tentative member of the group. I'd even seen hope flickering in the eyes of my club mates that, on one future miraculous Tuesday morning, I might become nice. I didn't plan to fulfill their longings anytime soon.

Our leader, Elsa, a retired school librarian, was a thin woman in her late fifties. She was holding her book in her lap and squinting at the wall, like she was puzzled by the novel's contents. This was how she always began. It was her way of trapping one of us into volunteering a stupid comment that the rest of us could pounce on and feed off.

Winnie, a deep thinker with a masochistic bent, took the bait.

"I don't think Gatsby knew who he was," she said. "That was his trouble."

Elsa said, "Don't you think we're all a little like that?"

Lily, set for life, piped up next. "The rich aren't like you and me. I think that was one of the main points Fitzgerald was making. The rich are in a category all by themselves. You have a different perspective when you are raised with a silver spoon in your mouth."

Anne decided she'd have a turn. "It's like us."

"How do you mean, like us?" Lily said. "All of us here aren't rich."

"I'm talking about the church," Anne said. "We're not like most people either."

"I think we're getting off track," Elsa said. "The subject of the church doesn't enter directly into the novel. So I don't think there is any point in juxtaposing the careless rich and the church."

Anne wasn't ready to concede.

"Most of us live in an ivory tower too," she said.

And then she busied herself by staring into her coffee cup. Elsa capped her wrath with a mild smile.

"What do you think, Jane?" Elsa said.

I decided to play.

"Gatsby knew who he was; he just wanted to live the fantasy of being someone else."

"Insightful," Elsa said. "Can the rest of us expand on that?"

No one felt like expanding.

Lily said, "What was that T.J. Eckleburg thing all about, you know, his eyes staring out from the billboard?"

"I think it had to do with the American wasteland," Winnie said. "You know, dreams not coming true."

"Insightful," Elsa said.

"Isn't it kind of like us?" Anne said.

"You're a broken record this morning, Anne," Winnie said.

"You know what I mean," Anne said. "We want to believe the church is a certain way, and we know it isn't."

"We're getting off topic again, I think," Elsa said.

I said, "I don't think we're off topic. Anne has a point. The church is an enterprise with the same rags-to-riches dreams as Gatsby. The difference is that we want God to sanction our dreams."

"Did you take first-year English in college?" Lily said.

"SparkNotes," I said.

"We wish you wouldn't always do that," Elsa said. "The whole point of the group is to provoke our thinking and stimulate ideas that we can exchange and in that way gain further insight into the books we are reading."

"Anne just had an original thought, and you said she was getting off track," I said.

"Let me explain to you again," Elsa said. "We have intentionally purposed to leave the church out of our discussions. We are broadening our view of the world so that we can relate in a more effective way to the people out there who don't share our beliefs. Literature is a way to close the gap between us and them. That is why we're not studying overtly Christian books. We are trying to be more inclusive and not so narrow-minded, which, as we all know, is the way we are frequently characterized by non-Christians. How can we be effective witnesses to the unsaved if we don't engage our culture? At the same time, we are not here to pick apart our church either. Do you understand the purpose of our club now?"

"I think the American Dream has had a lot to do with the rise of consumer churches," I said.

"I think so too," Anne said.

Elsa's face flushed, but before her steam blew, she remembered she was a Christian and only sputtered and rolled her eyes.

Lily came to the rescue.

"The green light at the end of Daisy's dock was a neat image. It symbolized, I think, the unattainable, an enchanted object that had no substance in itself, the same way Gatsby's vision of having a life with Daisy had no real substance in reality."

Lily's husband was big in retail. She had too much time on her hands.

"That is more like it," Elsa said. "That is exactly what I mean by reading the book with a critical eye, remembering the points we would like to make, and then coming together to compare our responses to the work. Do you see now that we don't need to have the church in everything?"

I said, "What do you think about that green light, Elsa?"

"Well, Lily has explained it nicely, I think. There's not much more to say."

Lily's cell rang. We flashed our annoyed faces at her; she answered it anyway. It sounded like it was her better half on the other end. She listened, and seconds later she shrieked.

"No, it can't be!"

Her eyes expanded, like they were ready to give birth. Then her mouth opened too, but nothing came out. She beeped off her hubby. Something more was up than a domestic squabble.

"What is it?" Elsa said.

"It's…it's…the pastor…" Lily said.

"What about the pastor?" Winnie said.

"They found him dead."

I said, "You mean Pastor Jessop? What happened?"

"No, not Pastor Jessop, Pastor Norman Parks, they found him floating in his swimming pool. They think he must have drowned."

"That just can't be," Winnie said.

Elsa closed *Gatsby*, pressed the book into her lap with both hands, and surveyed her little group.

"Oh my," she said.

Book club was over for the morning.

* * *

CHAPTER FOUR

I headed back to the office short one client. I wasn't fond of Norm, but he was dead now, and that tends to make you feel better about a person. Norm was short on scruples and long on ambition, although that described a lot of people. He was too young to go for the long swim. Death erased any opportunity for reform, and I suspected there was a lot more that Norm needed to reform before he left us than I and the church knew about. Hidden beneath his shining light, the odds were even he'd been adding illegal pursuits to his senior-pastor-in-waiting credentials, and that meant I was obligated to find out if he drowned or was flushed. When a person turned up dead, and it just so happened that the dead person had hired you to do a job, whether you were getting paid or not, your duty was to investigate. Besides, from a selfish point of view, losing a client at the beginning of a case hurt my pride.

I had a visitor waiting when I arrived at my door. Amy was pacing there.

"Why didn't you answer your cell?" she said.

"I thought it would be nice to talk to you in person."

"Don't try to flatter me. I'm not in the mood," she said.

"Let's go in. The neighbors can be nosy."

Amy followed me into my office like she was next up on *American Idol* and I was a stagehand standing in the way of her destiny. She was even more charming when agitated. I sat behind my desk and watched her vibrate. Before she buzzed away, I tried to make a connection.

"I used to be cute like you," I said.

"What happened?"

She tried to look interested as she waited to explode.

"The bloom faded. You might consider that before you waste your life pretending to be someone you're not."

"How insightful," she said. "But I didn't come here for girl talk."

She upped the volume and stomped her foot.

"It's my dad I'm concerned about. You don't think he had anything to do with it, do you?"

"What do you mean? I wasn't aware there was anything for your dad to have anything to do with. Do you have some information that might suggest Norman's death was anything other than accidental? If you do, I would like to hear it."

Amy was frustrated now.

She said, "Oh, come off it. You don't think it was an accident any more than I do. Norman had his faults, but he at least knew how to tread water."

"Have you talked to Sally yet?"

"Yes, of course, but she is half out of her mind."

Amy looked up at the ceiling and tapped her foot on the floor.

I said, "Do you think you might be able to sit down a minute? You're stirring up the air."

Amy pouted at me, arms akimbo, and then, sensing her rebellious act was pointless, acquiesced and flopped into my client's chair.

I said, "Until we hear the police report, we won't know if someone helped promote Norman to glory or whether it was an accident. So why don't we wait until then?"

"It wasn't an accident. I know it. I told you before. There was too much at stake."

"Is there something you're not telling me?"

"Norman had a few enemies, not just…What I mean is, my dad is better off with him gone, but Dad didn't think of him as an enemy. I mean, my dad wouldn't do anything like that. But there are a few others that I know of whose dislike for Norman has been raised to a new level lately."

I was dying to hear who the others were, but there was no sense looking under that rock unless it was established that Norm had taken his last swim with a little help from his brethren.

"Here's some advice for you," I said. "You need to back off, and calm yourself down, and wait to hear the police report. In the meantime, I'll talk to a friend of mine downtown and see what I can find out."

Amy reviewed my latest effort at reasoning and then tried to stare me down, her cute face doing its best to look severe. I played her game for a few seconds, and then my desktop became more fun to look at. Fortified by her staring victory, she was ready to make her point again.

"I'm telling you…Norman was murdered."

She folded her arms to signify *end of story*.

"I've noticed you seem to have a gift for getting at the heart of things. If you're willing, I might consider taking on a disciple. It gets lonely around here, saving the world all by myself."

"I would rather flip burgers."

"I'm glad we have an understanding. But while we're on the subject, since you're no longer employed as a pastor's kid, what else do you do?"

"If you must know, I'm between jobs. After I finished college, I put in a year at Vancouver Film School. But the business is slow right now."

"That's a tough racket. Are you sure it's the kind of thing a girl with your background should be involved in?"

"Yes, I'm sure, Mother. Any other questions?"

"As a matter of fact, I do have one. How does your dad feel about your career choice?"

"He's very supportive."

Annoyed, she then stood and posed for a snit commercial.

She said, "It's not like I'm making porn movies."

She observed her posture and, unimpressed with her own performance, decided she was leaving now. I was just as happy. Doorknob in hand, she turned back toward me.

"I'd like to hire you," she said.

"Hire me for what?"

"I want to protect my dad, and you already know some of our family history. I'll hire you to find out who killed Norman."

"Like I said, you're getting ahead of yourself. But if he was murdered, I'd be interested myself to find out who did it. Save your money for rent."

"Do you always have to be so superior?"

"It's become a habit."

"At least you admit it."

"I didn't say it was a bad habit."

Amy took her leave. I was left holding a bag of impure thoughts about the church and the people who ran it. I hoped Amy was wrong and Norman had only come up half a lap short on his race to the podium and not been torpedoed by a person or persons unknown. Either way, I knew I had to go back and have a few words with Sally. I wasn't looking forward to it.

On the phone Sally seemed anxious to talk to me about something and asked if I would come to see her the next day. She hoped the police would have concluded their business by then. When I caught the local evening news later at home, the police hadn't released any details about Norman's death, not even if foul play was suspected. Their account next morning was the same, just routine. The lid was clamped on tight for some reason, and the media didn't seem too nosy to find out why. But what was a dead pastor, more or less, compared to the bodies piling up from the gang wars? Our paradise by the sea was being invaded by the boys from hell, and there wasn't much that anybody could do about it. Vancouver's privileged position as a major port city made it vulnerable to traffic of all kinds. There was an Ecstasy plague infecting the continent from here, and there was no one around much interested in developing a vaccine.

My morning trip over to the North Shore was dismal. The drizzle had settled in. I ignored the guy in the police vehicle sitting in Sally's driveway. She answered the door before I rang. Pitiful brown eyes stared at me from a blank white face that matched the décor. By the way her legs faltered as she led me into her living room, I suspected she'd been drinking something stronger than tea. I sat in my favorite white leather armchair and tried to ignore the crime scene tape around the pool. Sally sat on the matching white sofa facing me. Her wrinkled black cotton dress absorbed some of the glare. Her anxiety had diminished since our phone conversation. She didn't offer me anything to drink. She then secured her sitting position by brushing flat the skirt of her funeral frock with the back of one hand. That accomplished, she cocked her head to the side for a few seconds and began to measure out an explanation of current events for my benefit.

Too composed to be real, she said, "You see, it's like this."

She sounded matter-of-fact, like it was the opening line of a long story that got a lot juicier later. Even though I already knew what *it* was like from my last visit, the least I could do was hear her version.

"I won't pretend," she said. "We haven't had an easy life."

I changed my mind about being kind. I didn't like the direction this was headed. I hadn't taken the trip up the mountain to hear the true confessions of a loveless marriage. Slapping her wasn't an option, so I tried a question instead.

"Did the police say what the cause of…?"

"There was blood," she said and sniffled. But her eyes were dry. "Sorry, it's the antidepressants. I shouldn't mix… never mind…you know…There was blood everywhere. Red in the pool."

Outside, the pool looked innocent enough, but there was nothing I wanted to see out there. I didn't want to be antisocial when it came to the police, but I'd stay out of their way this time and avoid the trouble.

"You found him?" I said.

"I went down to Park Royal to do some shopping, and when I got back…He must have come home while I was out and gone for a swim. He was naked. He liked to do that— the trees and the fence, no one can see in. When I arrived there was nobody else here, just Norman. I told the detectives that."

She looked around the room to make sure she was right, that there was nobody else here, and that she hadn't told a lie.

"And the blood, all the blood."

Sally's wide eyes searched the room's white carpet, like she feared traces of red had violated her sanctuary and were threatening to stain her white life.

Satisfied she was safe for now, she said, "He played around, you know. I wasn't supposed to know, and I pretended not to. What good would it have done? I didn't tell the police that, either."

"Either? What else didn't you tell them?"

"About Dad, of course. We need to protect him. He wouldn't do this, even if he was angry."

"If he didn't do it, we don't need to protect him. And what do you mean, *even if he was angry*? Is your dad angry often?"

"They had an argument on the phone a couple of nights ago. I overheard. You could tell they were both yelling, not just Norman. I didn't tell the police that. My dad needs a rest. And you need to help him, so the police don't find out and come to the wrong conclusion."

"It's safe to say, then, that in your opinion your dad and Norman's relationship wasn't ideal?"

"Yes, there is no doubt about that, but it wasn't that bad. It would never have come to this. Dad's not capable of doing something like this. And there is still that other matter about June. We don't want that to come out, either. You have to help."

"That's an easy one. Your dad and June aren't having an affair."

"You're sure? But what about…? Oh, I see. I should have known. Norman only wanted it to be true. Norman was like that. He wanted things his way. But not anymore."

I felt bad, not because she'd lost her Norman, but because I felt no sympathy for her. She was drowning too, but I didn't want to get involved. All I wanted were the facts. My heart was locked in its safe. I was relieved Sally had no interest in the combination, which spared me the effort of fabricating for her the appropriate emotions.

"What did the police tell you?" I said.

"They didn't need to tell me. Someone killed him. His head, it was coming from the back of his head. And they wanted to know where I was when it happened. Can you imagine? Me? Hitting him with a paddle and letting him drown?"

"A paddle?"

"There were two, for decoration, on the fence, canoe paddles. They took it away, the one that did it. I'm not going to pretend. Why should I pretend that I'm grieving? He was always doing it. He was always on it."

"Always on what?"

"The computer, those Web sites. Porn and chat rooms. I knew. He thought I was too stupid, a computer illiterate, but I'm not. And he met with some of them too. I knew."

Sally nodded her head; the decision was final. Justice had prevailed. Her God had fixed things for her. But I wasn't so sure she knew the right One. Hers approved of murder and romance novels and a world scrubbed clean as a backdrop for her righteous fantasies. So, husband Norm was even more complicated than I thought. In addition to his bounding aspirations to land upright in the senior pastor's chair, he was also an accomplished Internet body-surfer and chatroom enthusiast. But someone had decided he wasn't going to get away with his complexity anymore.

"Have you talked to your dad?" I said.

"I saw him yesterday. I went there. I wouldn't let him come here. He wanted to, but I convinced him. He's not well. They're bound to talk to him. He needs someone to protect him. He won't know what to do in a situation like this, not in his current state. Norman hired you to intimidate him, so now I'll hire you to keep him safe."

She was the second sister in two days who wanted to hire me. But I had no scruples about taking Sally's money, the not-so-grieving widow. The case was going to take more time now, and I was sure Norm was the kind of guy who had his insurance paid up. Sally would be rolling in it. The thought of doing it gratis for the good of the church family breezed right through my gray matter without stirring a ripple of guilt. Besides, I was feeling estranged.

"What is it that you are hiring me to do?"

"We need to find out who killed Norman, of course, and we need to protect my dad."

"I won't guarantee I can deliver on both of those needs. They might be contradictory."

"What do you mean? You don't understand yet, do you? There is absolutely no possible way that Dad had anything to do with Norman's death."

"If you say so, but either way I'll take the case. I charge a standard rate of forty dollars an hour, and since it's all in the family, I'll skip the retainer."

"The money's not an issue. The sooner you find out who did it, the less mess there will be for all of us, especially Dad."

Sally's white face cheered up. She sniffled into the lace handkerchief she had up her sleeve and then squeezed out a smile. She was making a phony show of being brave. She'd sobered a little too fast for my comfort, her will overriding the alcohol and prescription drugs. She had a stronger constitution than I thought, or she'd just had lots of substance abuse practice. Either way, she was holding together a little too well for an ivory tower Christian gal.

"I need to talk to your dad," I said. "But it wouldn't be a good idea to see him at his church office."

"No, that's right, you're wise. Meeting him there might raise suspicion. I'll call and let him know…He might not like the idea, but I'll insist he sees you. For his own good. I'll give him your number."

Sally was strengthening by the second. I'd misjudged her. Maybe her romance novels were only a front. But if that was the case, why didn't her sister Amy know that? My troubling guess was that Sally was complicated. She sniffled again, this time glancing over her shoulder and turning up her nose at the pool. Then she stood and waited for me to follow her lead. Since it was her house and she was now paying the bills, I took the hint. The interview was over. She showed me to the door to speed me on my way. I drove down the mountain again. The sun had gone missing; the thick black clouds vomited their projectiles. I thanked God for my Hummer.

* * *

CHAPTER FIVE

Sally arranged the meeting with Pastor Jessop. According to Sally's account, he'd been resistant to having fellowship with a private detective even if she was one of his flock. But after she'd showered him with pixie dust, the formula for which only daughters knew, he'd agreed to see me. I noticed on the way to his house that my road was littered with doubts. I tossed them at the trash can one by one. Some of them missed. Mercy would get me nowhere. Jessop lived in Point Grey, a respectable part of town, the old money oozing from the trees. There was new money competing in the area too. It had flown in when the well-heeled folks in Hong Kong feared they'd be pulling rickshaws after the Crown Colony reverted to China in '97. But the comrades in Beijing were smart enough not to upset the capitalist currency cart. In the meantime, the immigrants who had already flown the coop liked it here and didn't go back. They liked it so much they began to invite their friends to come on over, and the money kept coming. Then the Asian gangs infiltrated and started to compete for turf with the more traditional goons of European descent. But now that times were tough and the squeeze was on to control scarce resources, the gang boys, inspired by the example of the Mexican drug cartels, were popping each other off on a regular basis. That was bad for respectable business, so before the Winter Olympics came to Vancouver town, the girls at city hall made sure they didn't get their hair mussed with the whole world watching. They got behind a heavy push to clean up the mess and make the whole sweaty affair pleasant, Canadian style, eh? Their plan was to keep the tourists happy and feeling safe enough to empty their pockets here. The Mounties, dressed in their

public image scarlet tunics, had kept their horses tethered
outside the good-time-had-by-all saloon, but their plain-
clothes colleagues weren't that festive-minded. With the ter-
rorist threat to the Olympics thrown into the mix, security
had been tighter than a nun's thong. But now that the Olympics had come and gone, it was open season again.

Pastor Jessop agreed to see me at two o'clock. I was on
time, and the wrought iron gate was open. I drove through
the gap in the scruffy ten-foot-high cedar hedge and continued around the circular driveway to the front door. The
house was modest for the neighborhood, and he'd either fired
the gardener or the half-acre grounds had been the wife's
domain. Thick ivy enveloped most of the two-story stone
structure, and the cedar trees, in their old age, were growing
too close to the roof, providing a shady canopy for the moss
growing on the cedar shakes. The West Coast rain forest was
eager to reclaim its territory, in a century or two. The Asian
housekeeper answered the door, took my particulars, and led
me into his study. The room was dark, except for the light
coming from a brass desk lamp. The emerald green curtains
were drawn. He was sitting behind an oak desk. Behind him
was a wall of books. At least five of them he'd written. Law-
rence Jessop was a best-selling author. His insights into spiritual growth could be found in the Christian Living section
of your local Christian bookstore. In some church circles, he
was an important man. He half stood when I approached,
and leaned forward, his knuckles pressing into the blotter for
balance. Then he waved at the chair in front of his desk,
inviting me to sit. I thought I caught a leer slither my way
when I crossed my legs, but I wasn't sure if he was checking them out or was looking down, embarrassed to be in his
situation. As a concession to my beauty, he went over and
opened the curtains a few inches and then returned to his
red leather chair.

"I'm sorry, Jane," he said. "The light bothers my eyes. I haven't been myself lately. I need peace and quiet. Your name is Jane, isn't it?"

"Yes, Pastor…"

"Don't bother with the pastor title. Call me Larry."

I felt honored. He always looked impressive Sundays in the pulpit, almost elegant, but this afternoon his charisma was on crooked. He wore a burgundy tracksuit that looked like it was more for lounging in his delicate condition than for running a few laps around the neighborhood before dinner. His short silver-gray hair was combed forward and brushed up at the front. His face was thin under the trimmed white beard, but he was packing weight around the middle. A BMI chart might have accused him of obesity.

"All I wanted was some time to rest," he added. "And now this. Poor Norman. That's why you've come, of course. Sally informed me she hired you to find out who killed him. I am uncertain as to why that is necessary. It has been my understanding that murder investigations fall under the jurisdiction of the police."

"That's true, but your daughter also wanted me to make sure your interests are protected from any scandal that might arise."

"Scandal? I didn't know I was involved in any scandal. Perhaps you can enlighten me."

"Norman suspected that you and June Forsythe were having an affair. He hired me to catch you with your…I mean, to get the evidence, and he was planning to use the information he expected I was going to gather as a way of forcing you out of the leadership of the church. His strategy, of course, is of no benefit to him now, since he is no longer with us."

"Am I mistaken, or are you hinting that I might have had something to do with his death?"

"I understand that you and Norman have had heated arguments in the past."

"Sally must have told you that. Yes, of course we did. He was my son-in-law. The relationship was never perfect. But would you mind telling me if Sally was in agreement with Norman's plan?"

"She saw it as a way for you to retire in peace. She was thinking of your welfare."

"I see. I suppose she would be. But I wonder when she came to the conclusion that I wasn't able to look after my own welfare? Never mind, it's irrelevant really. I'm tired of the whole mess. There's no end to it."

Larry's face contorted, and his teeth clenched. He looked like he was warming up for a rant. He was.

"No, there's no end to it. You have no idea. If it isn't one thing, it's another. If it isn't different factions and backbiting in the congregation, it's immorality and marriages splitting up and the constant threat of the whole house of cards falling because of financial uncertainty in our chaotic world. And I'm supposed to carry it somehow. I have for years. And then there's the sheeps' favorite diversion, taking offense when their needs aren't met and church-hopping like Easter bunnies. Christians are nothing if not sensitive."

Larry had been telling his tale to his pen, which he twisted back and forth between the thumb and forefinger of his right hand. The pen was hard of hearing, so he shifted his focus to me and yelled, "It isn't even a traditional congregation anymore. There was a day when you were born into your denomination, and you stayed there for life. And we all believed the same way. Now we have the whole spectrum in our church, from fundamentalists to charismatics, all of them attracted to the flavor of the day, to whatever church is the most popular for whatever reason. They come because their friends do, or they come because the church has the best program to suit whatever their selfish need is. But it's our fault. We encourage them with our seeker-sensitive, purpose-driven shallowness. Forget the Cross; get results. Success is what counts. And now we need to cater to them so we can keep paying the bills. Nobody cares about character anymore."

Larry was losing it. His own character was weakening by the second. Letting true confessions slip to a common parishioner was discouraged in the best of church leadership circles. I doubted that his recent insights were found in any of his books. He needed a rest; his daughters were right about that. He pulled out of his nosedive, took a deep breath, exhaled, and resurrected his pastoral bent.

"How long have you been with us?" he said.

"I've been at your church about six months."

Larry relapsed.

"It's not my church; it's God's church, or at least it was. Now I don't know whose it is anymore, but it's certainly not mine."

His anger pangs were coming closer together. He relaxed again and found his pastor's voice, the soft, unreal one he must have learned years ago in pastor's school.

Sounding concerned, he said, "Didn't you come from back east?"

"I moved my business out here from Toronto after my father died. I had a growing interest to come."

Larry waxed nostalgic and said, "My first pastorate was in Toronto."

"So I understand," I said.

"And you never married?"

Pastors were nosy when it came to marriage, even when they were preoccupied with the end of the church as they knew it. I tried not to be offended and bit my tongue, preventing it from asking if he was only curious or if he liked what he saw.

"No, never," I said.

I'd resolved on the way over not to take any prisoners, so I aimed a shot between his caring, inquisitive eyes.

"Did you kill Norman?" I said.

Larry laughed. It wasn't insidious or maniacal. He laughed like my question had brightened his dark day.

When he stopped, he said, "Does Sally think I did?"

"If she does, she didn't tell me. She's more interested in protecting you."

"I know I shouldn't be making light of the situation, and I'm not. Your question caught me off guard. No, I didn't kill Norman."

Larry, almost old enough to be my father, leaned forward to take a closer look at me. He smiled. I felt violated, like he was taking an inventory of my soul. But I was confused. Was he looking for some action in there, or were his paternal instincts searching for another daughter to adopt? And if he tried to come closer, would I resist? A pastor for a suitor had to be an honor, but maybe not; he was an older one, and crazy besides. He sensed my confusion and backed off. I was relieved.

He said, "No, I actually loved Norman. He had his faults, and he was confused about authority and how one is promoted in the Kingdom of God, but he might have been redeemable, given another chance. That's not going to happen now."

Larry looked back down at his pen. It had nothing to add.

"Do you have any idea who might have wanted Norman stricken from the church roll?"

"It would be unhealthy for me, the pastor of the church, to speculate on that. Information that I might possess concerning matters of that kind is privileged. When I say that, I don't mean, of course, that I have any confidential information concerning Norman. However, I can divulge that Norman had a common character flaw, one that a lot of men have, and I was concerned it might lead to his downfall, but I never imagined anything like this."

I was too polite to ask him if *character flaw* was a tidy term used to cover over an oozing crevasse.

I said, "It's funny that he would suspect you of the same thing. For the record, is there any truth to the allegation your relationship with June Forsythe deserves a higher rating than siblings-in-the-Lord?"

"I am sad to hear that Norman hoped June and I were involved in an intimate way, but the idea is absurd. June and I have never had an adulterous interest in each other."

"Did you and Norman discuss his character flaw?"

"Yes, but it was awkward. He was never forthcoming, and because he was my son-in-law, I thought it inappropriate to press the issue."

"I don't want to belabor the point, but Sally said you and Norman had a heated discussion on the phone the night before he was dispatched to greener pastures."

Larry jumped up and began to pace behind his desk. He was off to the races again.

"That was about another matter entirely," he said. "This isn't an easy job. You have no idea. The board is preoccupied with money, the bottom line. There isn't a spiritually-minded one in the bunch. If it wasn't for the majority of people supporting me, they might easily find a reason to fire me. They can do that, you know. Norman has taken sides with them… I mean, he did take sides, for his own self-interest, not that they were planning to replace me with Norman. They would prefer someone less ambitious than he was. There's a lot of money involved."

Larry stopped pacing and returned to his seat.

"I don't know why I'm telling you this," he added.

I doubted that. Off the deep end or not, Larry was an intelligent man. He was no stranger to church politics, and he'd seen a lot of cash flow. He was letting me in on a few financial secrets for a reason, but I didn't know if he was pointing a finger at the board because he knew they were responsible for Norman's premature departure, or if he was misleading me for his own self-preservation. Either way, he wasn't fond of his board.

Larry relapsed again and pounded his fist on the desk, like he was having a Sunday morning flashback.

"The devil was behind it," he said. "He did it. I know he did. But it was my fault."

I wasn't surprised that Larry was willing to inform on his evil partner in crime, but I didn't expect him to implicate himself in the process.

I said, "You mean the devil killed Norman and you were his accomplice?"

Larry wasn't listening to me. He was nodding and at the same time pulling and turning the wedding band that he now wore on his right ring finger.

"He killed her," he said.

"Pardon? Who did he kill?"

"Cynthia's gone. None of this would have happened if she was still here."

"I see. I'm sorry. I misunderstood…You're talking about your wife being killed."

Larry came back from his inner journey and said, "That's what the devil does. Who else do you think goes around killing people?"

Since he was asking, I said, "Other people?"

"I spent more time with the church than I did with her. And now look."

I looked. He was right. His life wasn't pretty.

Silly compassion flickered to life and said, "I'm sure it wasn't your fault." Then I snuffed it out before it had a chance to spread.

"If you want to talk about adultery," he said, "I will tell you about adultery of the worst kind. I stole Christ's bride and made her my mistress to please myself. And Cynthia gave up competing with her. The church has been my mistress, and I compromised to keep her. But the devil isn't impressed with our compromises. When we compromise, then he just takes more. And now Cynthia is gone, and I'm left here suffering in a sinful relationship. I need to give her up, but I don't know how. If I do leave now, then a lot of good people are going to be hurt. The church is Christ's bride, not my harlot, or anyone else's. I reaped what I sowed."

The church and the devil's doings were fascinating stuff, but I hadn't dropped over for a sermon.

"Have the police been here to see you yet?" I said.

"They came yesterday. They wanted to know where I was when Norman died. They said it was routine."

"While we're on the subject, where were you?"

"I spent the afternoon here with June. Ironic, isn't it, considering Norman's plot?"

"Why did you meet here?"

"It's safer here, and more comfortable. We were going over the books. My office at the church is too much for me to bear right now, and we had some financial matters to discuss, things best talked about in private, away from the church staff. Church walls have ears."

Larry leaned his head toward me and cupped his ear to show me what ears did.

"According to Sally, Norman knew you spent time here with her. He followed you. Did you have a lot of financial matters to discuss, or were there other issues?"

"I can't tell you anything about our discussions. They are confidential."

Larry was positive of that. He'd decided to clam up. He was tired of the questions and exhausted from having to perform his sensitive portrayal of the beleaguered cleric. I'd had enough of our getting-acquainted session too.

"I would like to talk to you again, if that's all right. You might be able to help me further when I learn more about the circumstances surrounding Norman's death. And I know Sally would like us to keep in close touch, given her concern about your reputation."

Larry stood and began to show me to the door.

"That would be fine," he said. "But I don't know why Sally has such an obsession with my reputation. I have nothing to hide."

He extended his hand and attempted a smile that failed. I dismissed the thought that he expected me to kiss his pinkie ring and gave his soft but firm offering a shake.

"One other thing," I said. "Alec Brandish, he's your board chairman, isn't he?"

"He runs the business end," he said, unhappy I'd brought the subject up.

"Thanks, Larry, I hope we have the opportunity to talk things over again real soon."

Larry retreated behind his desk again.

He said, "If Sally had known the truth about June and me, she wouldn't have gone along with Norman's subterfuge."

"No, you're right," I said, and left him to his speculations.

Outside, the rain had taken a break. My Hummer waited for me to feed it some gas. I was happy to. Alec Brandish was my next stop, but it wasn't going to be easy getting in to see him. He was a busy man. He was the CEO of Brandish Corporation, a billion-dollar empire with its sticky fingers in everything from publishing to mining to electronics. Its share price had belly flopped in the recession, soaking its investors. If Brandish was in town, I'd take a shot at dropping in on him tomorrow. Right now I had a craving for Chinese. I took my usual route down to Chinatown. The sun was heading the same way, northwest toward the Coast Mountains, where it planned to hide out for the night. The clouds ran pink and orange and gold. It wouldn't be long before the scene faded to black, leaving the city lights to fend for themselves. According to the eggheads with the jumpy detectors, Vancouver stood on shaky ground. They said the Big One was coming one of these days. The earth's plates were plotting to jerk the ground out from under us, like a playful dinner guest unable to whip the tablecloth out fast enough, leaving the party's hosts to clean up the mess. If Mother Earth had been ready in time, it would have been an unforgettable Olympic event as billions of her fans watched her go for the gold, the perfect ten.

* * *

CHAPTER SIX

The next morning I tap-danced the sister-in-the-Lord routine for Mr. Brandish's secretary. She was wowed enough with my audition to give him a buzz, and he was willing to see my act in person. I figured his door had been pushed open by a call from Pastor Larry. After about five minutes, he waddled out in his black pinstripe suit to welcome me in. He looked like Jabba the Hutt with bad hair. He was about Larry's age, though the excessive padding made him look younger. He smiled at me, pretended to be jolly, and invited me into his ballroom. Everything was oversized and shiny, especially the chandelier. Alec gave me the seat of honor and then snuggled into his soft leather chair, parts of him spilling over.

I opened with, "Your office is big enough to be a gym."

Alec lost his jolly smile in the flabby creases. He now sat with his business face on, his hands folded and resting on his stomach's substantial top shelf.

"I have seen you Sunday mornings," he said.

"Not first thing, I hope."

Alec snickered. So did I.

"Of course, I don't get there every week," he said. "My company commitments require that I spend a substantial amount of my time overseeing our varied interests that we have established all over the globe. And I am dedicated to giving Brandish Corporation my personal attention. We here at Brandish are dedicated to serving our customers and shareholders with the highest degree of skill, competence, and integrity. And we discourage vigorously those who would try to cause any deviation from our goals."

Alec was reciting his public relations brochure and threatening me at the same time. That was a good sign.

"I know you're a busy man, so I won't keep you. I've been hired to do a job for Sally Parks. Part of it entails making sure Pastor Jessop's reputation isn't sullied as a result of the investigation into Norman's death."

"Yes, an investigation, I'm sure that's required," he said. "But don't you think we can take care of our senior pastor's reputation?"

The threat continued. He had the resources to destroy anyone he wanted, including me. If I caused trouble, he'd get out his flyswatter. I decided to buzz around the garbage heap anyway.

"How are the church finances these days?"

Alec didn't like the sound of that. The fat below his right eye twitched. I'd kneaded his dough in the right spot.

I added, "I'm asking as a contributor to the church, of course."

"The church has an annual general meeting to discuss financial matters. The last one was February eighth."

"I must have been home rearranging my lingerie drawer."

"Perhaps you won't be so busy next year. Is there anything else I can help you with? You must have come for a reason."

Alec then puckered in thought, offering me his innocent lighter side. My guess was that he thought he looked cute. He didn't.

"Yes, there is one other thing. I would like to know your opinion of Pastor Jessop's health."

"Is this a personal concern of yours, or does your question pertain to Norman's death and Sally's concern for her father's reputation?"

"I'm asking how much longer you think he will be around."

Alec stood and, doing his best penguin impersonation, came around and leaned in on me, plopping his ample derriere on the front of his desk.

He said, "As long as he wants to be...unless, of course, there are other unforeseen circumstances."

I heard the threat again, this time combined with a hint Alec was about to become playful. He wasn't my type, even with his pockets on. I saw an image of him swallowing me, my pretty legs left kicking out between his lips. I had an urge to escape from his sphere of influence. I didn't want to give him time to discover that my brave front had sagged. I made my move. This time he took me all in with his eyes as I stood and retreated. No more hiding his intentions; they blazed on his jowls.

"Thank you for your time," I said. "I'll be in touch."

"I'd like that," he said and licked his lips.

From the hunger in his eyes, I'd expected at least a drool.

Alec had no fear. Why would he? Nobody would believe me, and if they did, they wouldn't take my side against him. If he came any closer, I had my martial arts training up my sleeve, but I'd be reluctant to risk getting my hand stuck in his lard.

"That's no way to talk to a sister in the Lord," I said.

"Yes, I do like to think of us as one big happy family."

"Don't you think lechery is passé?"

Alec cooled.

"I do hope you realize you are out of your league. I'm going to make an exception this time, because we have our church in common, and because I do like the way you handle yourself. So here's some good counsel, free. Let the police handle the investigation, and as far as Pastor Jessop's future is concerned, you would be well-advised to let Sally know he is in good hands with us."

"Thank you for taking the time to see me, and for being so generous with your free advice. You have restored my faith in church leadership."

Alec filled his lungs and blew the air back out, like he was bored with his birthday candles. His pout let me know he was disappointed with me. I was happy for him to feel that way. He launched his rear and staggered a step closer. He tried his smiling Mr. Nice Guy on for size, but it was a bad fit. His evil was hanging out.

He said, "Remember, there is too much involved in this for you to handle. Stick to divorce cases and retrieving children abducted by their parents. I like you the way you are. I especially like the way you move."

I tried to be Christian about it and return the compliment, but I knew it wasn't nice to lie.

Instead, I said, "Thanks again for your time."

"I would be willing to give you more of it, if you were agreeable for us to get together under different circumstances."

"That sounds delightful," I said. "I'd love to meet your wife."

I made my getaway and rode the elevator down. Maybe there were legitimate reasons why Brandish turned out the way he did—maybe he had a tough childhood, maybe he was an orphan, maybe he was abused—but that didn't let him off the hook. Most of us had tough childhoods, but the majority of us turned out less greasy. I was satisfied with our

little talk. He'd told me what I'd wanted to know, though he
didn't seem worried that I knew it. There was plenty of foul
play going on, and the church board was up to its apse in it.
What Norm's passing had to do with church finances was
the question. The Sunday gospel message and the weekly
programs were one thing; the income from eight thousand
tithing members and what was done with the overflow was
another. And it was clear Brandish was running the show.
Pastor Jessop, even in his former days of a sound mind, was
no match for Alec the Great. It was easy to see that Brandish and his ways were the direct cause of Jessop's current
condition. Brandish was a wolf in a fat suit. Big bucks and
slippery administration were running the church, not Jessop
and the associate pastors. They were only the hired hands,
kept around to feed the flock. The flock's role was to keep
the money coming. It was a business, but times were tough.
Many of the ordinary folks had been laid off, which hurt the
weekend take, and now even the rich folks in the rich congregation were hurting. So far this year, the balance sheet's bottom line, posted on the board for all to see as a stimulus for
giving, showed that offerings were down. As for the church's
holdings, a new development for well-to-do seniors was in
the works at Whistler Village, capitalizing on the hype left
over from the Winter Olympics. And who stood to benefit
the most, or lose the most, if the deal went south due to trick-
ling cash flow? I knew one thing for sure. Jesus had nothing
to do with any of it.

I rode with the windows rolled down on the way back to
my office. I was counting on the breeze to blow away Brandish's residue, in case I'd gotten any on me. He made my
dear father look good. Before I turned onto the Bad Memory Lane route, my cell interrupted my pity thoughts. There
was a guy on the other end. And not just any guy. He was
the handsome, strong, silent type I'd seen at church Sunday
mornings. Last week he'd taken the time to introduce himself. He pretended that bumping into me at the coffee and

snacks table in the lobby after the service was accidental. I felt the spark. His name was Bert. I thought Bert was a funny name for a guy who looked like he did, but I didn't laugh in his face. It was too sincere to be mocked. He was about my age, tall, black hair, a touch of gray at the temples, dark complexion, a permanent five-o'clock shadow, and brown puppy dog's eyes. But could he cook? And now he was on my cell asking me if I wanted to go out for dinner Friday night. I couldn't think of anything smart to say, so I said *yes*. I'd keep my tongue locked for now, and if necessary I'd let him have it later. My response made him happy. I felt pretty good about it too and hung up. He'd changed my day, along with my mood. I felt cleaned off. Bertrand was a classy name. But maybe *Bert* was short for *Albert*. I hadn't done any investigating, though I did learn from the church gals on the hunt he was fair game and that his last name was Smith. He was a lawyer, but who was I to be choosy?

My office waited in its chronic delicate condition, whimpering for attention. I refused to give it any. I booted up the beast for a few games of Spider Solitaire, two suits. I needed time to think. There was a lot going on in my life and no one to talk it over with. God was there, but I hadn't been returning his calls. He and I had been on a different wavelength for a while now. I'd get back to him when I ran into something I couldn't handle myself. Although, there was no doubt Brandish was a handful. More than a handful, he was a bucket of trouble. But I would see how far I could go solo. I hoped to go the distance so I'd be there to see him get his reward. Little old me would expose his ugly insides for the world to see. His billions would be stacking up without him after I proved his thugs had popped off poor lust-filled Norm. Poor Norm. The media continued to remain silent on the details of his death. They were playing it like he was a drowning victim. A smell was rising. It looked like a cover-up. Alec had a few things to cover up too. Most people knew that pornography was hidden in Brandish Corporation's publishing portfolio, but Alec's personal involvement was glossed over when the subject came up among the faithful, like he wasn't responsible somehow. A corporation did what it did. The shareholders had to be satisfied. Bottom line. The word in the pew was that Pastor Jessop had been known to preach against pornography in his younger, fiery days. The fire was quenched now. The message was cold. My sources reported that enterprising Alec also had a green thumb, and he'd used it to hitch a ride on British Columbia's six-billion-dollar-a-year cash crop, marijuana. Brandish Corporation had friends in high places too, and I knew that if I continued to poke at Alec's corporate pus, my life wasn't worth a roach clip with a broken spring. But what else did I have to do?

A softer alternative came to mind. It was Bert with the brown eyes. He looked too good to be true. I didn't mind getting my feet wet, but if I was going to go for a swim, I needed to know where the rocks were and if there were any undercurrents. I didn't want to be discovered washed up in my birthday suit, no matter how lovely I looked. I'd go for warm and fuzzy to begin with and then try to keep it that way. Conflicts were to be expected later, and they would all be his fault. I was getting ahead of the game, but from past experience, I'd learned if you didn't pay attention to present details, you stood to lose down the road. But maybe I'd just run on instinct instead. Why not? Down deep I was as eager for romance as those innocent sixteen-year-olds I'd seen in church, whose dreamy eyes see only pink rose petals and rainbows and whose lips have never been kissed.

The phone interrupted my two-game streak. It was Amy. She skipped the pleasantries and went straight to it.

"You know as well as I do by now that my dad didn't have anything to do with it."

"You mentioned before that Norman had other enemies. Would you care to elucidate?"

"What do you mean other enemies? My dad wasn't his enemy."

"I stand corrected, but now how about it?"

"So all of sudden you don't care if we talk about it on the phone?"

"You're right, but not Digby's this time. I'll buy you lunch at the White Spot on Georgia. That's near your place."

"You've been checking into where I live, Mother?"

"I can read a phone book."

"Okay, one o'clock? I hope you can afford it."

Amy left me to reflect on my finances. I had to thank my dear father for that much. He'd left me his bundle. He'd saved his pennies, and, when he departed, I was set for life, as long as I didn't start playing the horses or hanging out in the casinos. He'd given up those entertainments himself in his younger years—bless his departed, twisted soul—after my mother had suffered enough, and from then on he deposited his loot in the bank. Now I could pick and choose the kind of depravity I wanted to involve myself in.

The restaurant rattled with the dwindling lunchtime crowd. Amy hadn't arrived yet. The chick who sat the diners obliged me with a booth for two. Sipping an iced tea, I waited for the princess to make her entrance. She slipped in about ten minutes later, her superior self above it all.

"You're looking mellow today," she said.

"I might have a reason to live," I said.

"Is he old enough for you?"

"There's no need to get snotty."

Working Her Way Through College came and took our order. We ordered salads, tributes to our willpower, and a bottled water for Amy.

"So what's your story this time?" I said.

"I don't make up stories. Do you want to hear about Norman's troubled acquaintances or not?"

"Is Brandish one of them?"

Amy looked impressed. I'd scored one for the middle-aged.

"You've done your homework," she said. "Did you learn your tough discipline at private eye school?"

"My father had his way of doing things."

"There you go talking about your father again. You must miss him. You didn't tell me how he died?"

Amy pasted sincerity on her face. I went along.

"If you have to know, his prostate finally got him."

Amy raised both eyebrows and pouted. She'd heard enough.

Relieving her embarrassment, I said, "What got Norm?"

Amy softened her voice to deliver her prepared speech.

"My former brother-in-law would have done anything to become senior pastor of the church. That was his dream. But it wasn't just my dad who was in his way. You mentioned Brandish. He's a dangerous man. And if Norman replaced Dad, that would have been more trouble for Brandish. Norman wouldn't have been content just to run the spiritual end of the church and let the board take care of the rest, the way my dad did. Norman wanted to take more of an interest in the financial end of things. In other words, he wanted to get his hands on more of the cash flow."

Amy waited, indifferent to my response. She glanced out the window and then looked around the restaurant, like she'd only offered me her opinion on this year's hemlines.

"Where did you get your information?" I said.

She aborted her disinterested act and said, "I don't need to tell you that."

"Where were you the afternoon Norman died?"

"You've got to be kidding me," she said. "I'm glad I didn't hire you, if this is the best you can do."

"How bad did you want to protect your dad? And what about Sally? You girls were both unhappy with Norman."

"Oh, great, a conspiracy theory. I thought you were working for my sister, not trying to cause her more grief."

The chick brought the bottled Dasani. Amy, in her huff, forgot to say thank you.

"It's my job to cover all the angles. Norman's life insurance would likely keep you girls swimming in lattes until the Lord comes back. How's the job hunting coming?"

"I'm going to ignore your nasty attitude this time," she said.

Amy was an expert on attitudes. I felt privileged she was going to ignore mine.

She said, "There's a weak link on the board, Sam Braithwaite. If you talk to him, you might get some idea of what's going on. Just leave my dad out of it."

"Is there any other interest you have in Norman's death, besides keeping your dad spotless, I mean? You seem eager to see the plug pulled on the church. Is there any reason for that…a reason I should know about?"

"Hypocrisy is too easy a target," she said. Amy let her mask drop. I caught a flash of the angelic little girl rising. "But church isn't supposed to be the way it is," she added.

That was different. I liked Amy when she was real. She did have a heart.

"It's a huge mess," she said. Then the left side of her frown quivered, and her tough self demanded she regain control.

To hasten our descent from the church's spiritual challenges to its earthly ones, I said, "A paddle in the back of the head isn't exactly a professional hit."

Amy leaned toward me, and in her Sunday-best insincerity said, "I feel so honored that you're sharing your keen detective insights with me."

The chick with the salads intervened and dropped them in front of us. Mine was the Mediterranean. She had the chicken Caesar. We said our own grace.

On the way back to my office, the sun tried to make a show of being at the center of things. The tricky clouds had other ideas. I stopped at a red light and admired my carbon footprint reflection in a storefront window. I'd bowed to the browbeating of the global warming elite and resisted buying a new Hummer. I'd make do with the one I had. I felt good about myself. My lunch with Amy had been more than a nice time; she'd given me a legitimate lead, bless her soul. She was a spirited child, and I was positive now that she had never been spanked, at least not by her parents. The proverbial *spare the rod and spoil the child* had been deleted from their parenting philosophy. That was a good thing in Amy's case. Their scriptural fudging had spared them a few visits from Child Services. Amy had plenty of life in her, and she would have given any instrument of punishment a run for its money. And if she were to let the little girl I glimpsed out to play more often, she'd be delightful. I had to watch she didn't get under my skin in a good way. She had the potential to disturb my emotional life, and who had time to deal with that kind of thing? My emotions were already filled to capacity, bubbling with my anticipation of Bert. But I hoped she'd make it through her crisis of faith. As for Sam Braithwaite, I'd seen him shuffling the offering plates Sunday mornings.

He was in charge of counting the beans in the back room, assisted by an understudy and a sturdy calculator.

The gray sedan had been following me since I left the restaurant. I wasn't positive that it was at first, but my erratic, convoluted trail hadn't flicked it off. Its intention was to be a companion of mine. I was okay with that, unless it was an amateur stalker. In that case, I wasn't so flattered. My guess was that Brandish had taken an interest in my daily activities and ordered a flunky to guard my body for future reference. I must have so impressed him that he couldn't bear to let me out of his sight. But was he planning to play rough after only one meeting? I could hardly wait to see.

My tail parked itself across the street from my office. I went in to freshen up a bit before I tackled Braithwaite. The rough ride through traffic had ruffled my feathers. After a few adjustments, I looked stunning again and ready to ask a few questions. The secretary at the accounting firm of Braithwaite & Stengel put me on hold so she could inquire if her boss was in. He was. I felt blessed.

"Is there something I can do for you, Ms. Sunday?" he said.

There was a hint of false self-assurance in Braithwaite's voice. It sounded like Brandish had been there ahead of me and told him to present a transparent and helpful front if I should happen to call.

"Not much. There's no cause for concern," I said.

"I'm not concerned, Ms. Sunday. Or is there something I'm not aware of?"

I pictured Sam on the other end, a short, slight man in his forties, in his spiffy black suit, his tie too thin, his mustache looking like it had been drawn with an eyebrow pencil. With a couple of twirls sketched on the ends, he'd have made the grade as a silent-film villain.

"Your firm keeps track of the church's finances, doesn't it?"

"That's right. We have been honored to offer our services to the church for many years now."

"Do you know how the seniors' project at Whistler is coming?"

"That's beyond my purview here at Braithwaite & Stengel. You would need to contact the church directly, or more specifically, you would have to address your inquiry to the church board."

"You sit on the church board, don't you, and you are the one in charge of the tithes and offerings?"

"Yes, but I'm not authorized to answer impromptu questions. As I said, you would be well-advised to direct your questions to the board, or more specifically, to Mr. Brandish."

"There's something fishy going on, and the death of Norman Parks has added to the stink. Are you planning to go down with the ship?"

"It just so happens that I have extensive nautical training, and it is extremely unlikely that I would sign up to sail on an unsound vessel, let alone go down with it. But I really can't talk any more right now. I know you think you have legitimate reason to pursue the course you are taking, but you aren't aware of all the facts."

"Do you mean there are more facts to be aware of? I like facts. In fact, I'm all ears to hear them."

"As I said, I have other matters to attend to right now. Good day, Ms. Sunday."

He left me to imagine my own facts, but he didn't know I had an unhealthy imagination. I imagined that Braithwaite & Stengel, inspired by the vision of Alec Brandish, was up to its abacus in money laundering. Cleanse your soul and your money, one-stop church shopping for the insiders. The government allowed churches to buy and sell property, for nonprofit purposes, of course. Pastor Jessop's church had been buying property, and selling it too, but Jessop was only a pawn in the church board's game. Brandish was the king of the finances. A barrelful of tithes and offerings had gone into buying and developing the seniors' center at Whistler Village. That expensive piece of real estate had to fit into the puzzle somewhere. And what were the selfish interests that Norm had been indulging in to provoke the board to submerge him in life everlasting? I was in the mood to find out.

* * *

CHAPTER SEVEN

Friday morning I took a ride down to the Lower East Side. I'd volunteered for service at the food bank. East Hastings Street wasn't pretty. It gave skid rows everywhere a bad name. When I first saw the food bank notice on the church bulletin board requesting help, my immediate thought was to donate a few dollars, or maybe more than a few, to keep my conscience from poking me in the heart and to keep the drugged and unwashed at a distance. I'd seen enough of the downside of life in Toronto. But I knew no matter how much money I donated, my conscience was going to do some poking anyway.

My job was to pack hampers, and if I passed that test, I was told there might be an opening later washing dishes in the soup kitchen. Many of the people who staggered in had missed a turn somewhere in life and found themselves in a dead end. They were the strung-out hard core. But many of the others were the working poor who needed food hampers to supplement their income and feed the kids. And then there were those working the system. Next to me on the assembly line of four was a reformed biker I'd seen at church. Stan Sommers was the kind who never missed a Sunday. One morning I overheard him telling his salvation story to a couple in the lobby after the service. He gave the play-by-play of the main event in his life as often as possible, to anyone who took the time to listen. He was zealous for God and devoted to Jessop, who had rescued him from his former life in the drug trade. Jessop had a prison ministry for years, and that's where he met Stan, who was doing time for possession and trafficking. Stan owned his own painting business now, but when he wasn't working on a job, he was helping out around the church as a handyman. And now this morning, I'd discovered that volunteering at the food bank was another one of his gigs. I wasn't sure he recognized me from church, but either way I could see he was impressed with my chic slumming outfit.

"You look too classy for this kind of work," he said.

I tried to appear flattered and too naive to hear the sarcasm.

He said, "I'm here every Friday."

He wasn't bragging about his charitable bent, only stating a fact. Stan was about fifty with thinning, blond, wavy hair. He was a wiry 5'10". His jean jacket vest had a Cross patch on one lapel, and the crest on the back read: Holy Riders. His black T-shirt clung to his gnarled biceps, and his forearms were tattooed. He looked like a poster boy for street-level crime. But he was clean now.

He paused his packing to answer my staring.

"That's the motorcycle club I'm in. We ride as many weekends as we can. We're like a church. We ride for the Lord. Before that, I was riding on the highway to hell."

Having summarized once again the motivation for his life, he resumed packing. I'd met his type in Toronto, minus the conversion experience. They weren't the kind of people you wanted to provoke, but Stan had changed his ways. I filled a few more boxes with the staples people needed to live on. I didn't see any gourmet Chinese, but there was bulk rice. Stan continued to keep his nose to the task until he remembered to relate a postscript to his story.

"I came to the church to help Pastor Jessop," he said. "What are you doing there?"

He took a step toward me, like a kind vegetarian vampire looking for an answer.

"I've got interests there too," I said.

He seemed satisfied with that and returned to his packing station.

A minute later, without looking up, he said, "I hope it works out for you…and that nobody I know gets hurt."

That was the end of our Christian fellowship for the morning. I was just as happy. I finished my packing duties and left. Riding my Hummer back uptown, I settled on the exact amount to give to the food bank.

* * *

He picked me up at seven, tall Bert with the brown eyes. He drove a Beemer. We were going to the theater and then for a late snack. He was playing Christian music on his sound system. I would have preferred something classical, Vivaldi maybe, on a first date, but it was his car, and I didn't want to get pushy. He had a real nice feel about him, soft and mellow, like he might be disturbed by a nuclear explosion, but not for long. He lived in a lovely dark cloud highlighted by tints of blue and set off by his graying temples. I sensed he planned to invite me in for a visit. How long I stayed depended on how much of a disturbance I caused. There was a chance he needed some disturbing, and I was positive I was ready for some mellowing out. Compromise was possible. My guess was his Barker Blacks were size twelve.

"Have you been a Christian for long?" he said.

Oops. I didn't like where this was headed. I cancelled my sarcastic response and took the change-of-subject option.

"Hmm, for a while," I said. "What kind of law do you practice?"

Bert glanced at me and smiled.

I said, "The gals at church told me about your shady occupation. They've compiled a lengthy profile."

"My area is civil law. I work for the attorney general's office, legal services branch. It's probably pretty dull compared to your line of work."

He smiled at me again and added, "I made some inquiries too. It beats Internet dating."

"I haven't tried that. I'm afraid of viruses. What about you?"

"No, I haven't tried it either. I'd rather meet people in the flesh."

I liked the sound of that. So did he. We had an understanding.

We took in the musical *Altar Boyz*, playing at the Arts Club. I enjoyed the way we sat there, close together. Our arms nudged and nestled for the first few numbers, and then he got bold and took my hand. I didn't bother resisting. Why would I? We were mature adults, and Christians too. We played like that for ninety minutes without an intermission. The show was good too. Later, I talked him into Chinese, and we had a smorgasbord in a little joint on Hastings. I hadn't purred in a long time, but I felt the subtle excitement coming on. The vibrations weren't just from the MSG. On the ride home, he obliged with Mozart. The atmosphere was thick, and when we spoke, it was filled with sparks. I had a decision to make when we got to my town house door. After we dawdled there a minute, he kissed me like he meant it, and then he made the decision for me. He said goodnight and hoped we'd do this often. I nodded my best nod, impressed by his restraint. I watched him drive away, and I reflected on the seriousness of sharing air, not to mention saliva. We'd made a covenant. I could live with that. Most men would have tried to gain entry. He must have known I wasn't that kind of girl.

Sunday came. I made the sacrifice and elbowed myself out of bed. The whole gang was at church for the second service, Jessop and his girls, Brandish and Braithwaite, and the book club gals. Bert beside me was a treat. The five-thousand-plus crowd was in communal mourning for Norm. Even the plastic flowers on the platform were hanging their heads. The worship team led us in a thudding blend of contemporary choruses and traditional hymns, culminating in "I'll Fly Away," in honor of Norm. Tears flowed. I hoped his wings were up to the trip. Pastor Jessop had opted to give the sermon this morning and struggled with the concept of many mansions in our Father's house. It was a warm-up for the afternoon. Norm's memorial service was scheduled for 2:00 p.m., when mourners would be exhorted to celebrate, knowing that Norm was now in a far better place. Jessop stumbled through his scattered message, his sensitive condition evident but attributed by most in the congregation to his love for his dearly departed son-in-law. I admired Sally for taking the trip down the mountain. She and Amy sat in the front center pew. Amy had abandoned the boys in the back row this week to come forward and comfort her sister. In the section to their right, Alec's gluttonous spread settled in the front row. His attempt to project warmth and understanding, when he turned his head to display his grief to his brothers and sisters, failed to disguise his contempt for those gathered, the corner of his mouth unable to break out of its sneer. Jessop finished his message; either that or he just decided to stop. Jessop had made his living talking, but now it seemed he'd lost his place. One of the deacons took over and gave instructions for the afternoon's main event. The service ended with "Amazing Grace." That was the truth. Bert and I skipped the refreshments in the lobby. We were hoping to catch a fall picnic between raindrops. I'd become domestic all of a sudden and even had a basket and blanket in the car. On the way out, I stopped to use the washroom. Amy was there rearranging herself. I talked to the girl in the mirror.

"Your dad did his best this morning," I said.

I expected some kindness from Amy in return for my peace offering. I was disappointed.

The sniffling girl in the mirror talked back at me.

"You've figured it out finally, then? No more conspiracy theories?"

"You look pretty in black," I said.

"Did you ask Braithwaite where all that money is coming from for their Whistler Village project?"

"But then you'd look pretty in anything."

"You're even smugger now that you've got Mr. Tall, Dark, and Handsome escorting your bones."

"Are you proud of me?"

"You're a winner, Mother."

I finished my mission and rejoined Bert in the lobby. Outside, the chivalrous sun was warming up to shine on our picnic. We sailed through town and into Stanley Park, my tail behind us. Bert didn't notice, and I didn't tell him. I hoped Brandish wouldn't be jealous. Second Beach was our destination. We parked our blanket on the grass, away from the concession stand. Kids controlled the area. I conceded to my better self that they had to be somewhere. I unpacked the basket. I felt so girlish I could have died. Before settling in and getting cozy, my insecurity arose from where I last stashed it.

I said, "You're not just looking for a private investigator, are you? For some secret intrigue of yours?"

"No, the phone book's full of private investigators. While we're on the subject, do you have any idea why that gray sedan has been following us?"

"He's a secret admirer, one of many. Maybe he'd go for three-way Frisbee."

"Do you carry a gun in that basket?"

"You know we're not allowed to carry guns in this country. Forget about him. It's a case I'm working on. Explaining will spoil the afternoon."

"Has it got anything to do with Norman's death?"

"I'm not on the stand, am I?"

"I'm not that kind of lawyer."

Bert made a move. I was in the mood to lie down anyway. I almost didn't care that he knew Norm's death was murder. Snuggling in the sunlight soothed my nerves. I didn't care what the kids in the park thought either. Our relationship was on the fast track.

"I love your perfume," he said.

The scent was my Regenerist cream, but why spoil the magic? Then Bert's attention turned from lovely aromas and clamped on to a somber thought.

He said, "My life was a total train wreck."

I didn't want to know about wrecks of any kind, but true confessions were about to be spilled. I hoped they wouldn't splash all over me and ruin my day.

I said, "Are you sure you wouldn't like something to eat now?"

I'd tried to stop it, but the train wreck story was hurtling down the track.

"No, I would rather talk for a while," he said, "if that's okay with you."

"If we must."

"Did I mention I like everything about you?"

That was a new one. I wanted to disagree and say he didn't know everything about me, but I enjoyed the illusion too much to ruin it.

He said, "And if we are going to continue our relationship, and I am extremely hopeful that we are, I think it would be fair to fill you in on some of my history."

On our first date we hadn't talked much. That had been perfect. Now he was insisting that we go to stage two, displaying and poking at our complicated, sad lives. I sat up and waited for the rest of his story, my nerves resuming their jangle. On a calming mission, one of his hands took the liberty of massaging my back. Off in the distance, the gray sedan lurked.

"I don't absolutely have to, if you would rather not," he said.

Bert was sensitive. My resistance to spilling our mutual guts wasn't strong enough to risk hurting his feelings.

"No, let's get to it," I said. "I know transparency is essential if one is going to have a relationship."

"Your clever tongue doesn't discourage me, Jane. As a matter of fact, I love it because it's part of who you are."

Oh, oh, he'd said the word, even if it was only directed at one of my parts. My heart hiccupped. Scary business was on the way. His intentions were honorable. He was looking for something long term. I had a choice to make, get to know him—or not.

He said, "I lived the big-shot lawyer playboy life. I never married. You can imagine."

"I could imagine, but I'd rather not. Are you still in the playboy mode, or have you moved on?"

Bert laughed. I liked that. My nerves relaxed enough to let me smile.

"I've reformed," he said. "Pastor Jessop had a lot to do with it. He showed me the light. I owe him my life. Now I'm looking for someone to share the rest of it with, someone who's been around."

We were beginning our first fight. He didn't know it yet.

I said, "How far around do you think I've been? Do you mean I've been around far enough that I'm on par with you and that I'm not too good for you?"

"I didn't mean it that way."

"I'm sorry I missed Norman's funeral now."

I was ready to abandon the blanket and basket and leave him there to reflect on his sins. Instead, I decided to get right down to it.

"How did you know that Norman was murdered?"

"Pastor Jessop and I are still close. You know, you're even more exciting when you're mad."

Bert was a sweet-talker. I bought his response and collapsed on the blanket. I needed a rest from the continuing battle.

He said, "What I was trying to tell you is that I'm positive we're a perfect fit."

"Not so fast."

He got a little freer with his hands, but not so free that we might corrupt the kids in the park. I was happy to know I wasn't too old or jaded for this. Sweet, chirping romance reared its devious head. To slow the proceedings, I blurted my confession. Since he'd played his hand, I figured I should lay mine down.

"I'm a little sensitive about having been around. I had a child when I was twenty. I gave her up for adoption. The father had been around too. Our relationship was short and not so sweet. I imagine he's still going around. I haven't heard from him since."

Bert got emotional and teary-eyed.

He said, "That must be rough. Do you know where she is now?"

"Yes, she's in Vancouver. But she's made it clear that she doesn't want any contact."

Bert's reaction to the subject of my daughter was digging up my buried heartache. I felt like bawling. My emotions were jumping around like those of a fourteen-year-old with deep-seated acne.

"How did you find out where she is if you weren't supposed to have any contact?"

"I don't really need to answer that, do I?"

"Oh, right, I see. But maybe she'll change her mind when she gets older. They do sometimes."

"There's no point. She's better off."

I didn't believe what I was saying. Neither did Bert.

"I doubt that," he said. "She's missing out on the opportunity to have a relationship with a lovely person. I'm planning to…if you give me a chance and let me in?"

"Go easy now. We both know by now how deadly closeness can be."

"We're already close, but if you need some space, I'll back off a little."

He squeezed me a bit tighter, which was fine with me.

"You're serious about this?" I said.

"You can't escape."

"I can render you helpless with my little finger."

"I would enjoy that."

"How about a ham and cheese sandwich instead?"

"I'll settle for that, for now."

The rest of our picnic proceeded without incident, unless you counted the extended period in the parking lot, in Bert's Beemer, getting acquainted in a chummy, snuggling kind of way and not caring what the guy in the gray sedan thought, either. And to round out my day, I was proud to discover my new beau's name was Bertrand.

* * *

CHAPTER EIGHT

Monday morning came with a bang. It was Braithwaite's partner, Stengel, on the phone. He talked like he was stifling vomit. He wanted to meet me, but not anywhere his stratum of society might congregate. I recommended Benny's Pool Room on West Broadway. Chances were nil that any of his kind would be loitering there. I suggested we meet when the doors opened at eleven. He gurgled his agreement to the place and time. So, Amy's lead had proved useful. I'd poked Braithwaite, and Stengel had squealed. I'd already done my homework on their accounting firm. Their last few years together had been strained. In recent months Benjamin Stengel had left his partner the job of serving the bottom line alone. The word was that Mr. Stengel's health had seen better days. From the sound of him on the phone, his life would soon be in the red.

Benny's Pool Room was a holdover from the sixties. Its location downstairs, below the Wishing Well Restaurant, sealed the dark in and natural light out. I'd learned from its regulars that Slick Benny, the founder of the tomb, shot his last game of eight-ball in '91. The current owner, Slow Bob, took over from Benny. He'd been riding his dead horse ever since. When the BC liquor laws loosened, he got a break, and the added income kept his impossible dream alive. The nonstop money game in the back room tossed a few more bucks his way, but not enough to keep him in mouthwash. On my way there, I didn't bother to lose the gray sedan. He was company. The woman on my Hummer's radio had a news flash for me. She said police were calling the death of

Pastor Norman Parks a homicide, but they had no suspects in the case at this time. I had a few.

Stengel was there when I arrived. He sat at a table in the area partitioned off for dining, where patrons were invited to enjoy Bob's specialty, cheeseburger and fries, a delicacy he prepared without reference to the fundamentals of FOODSAFE. Bob leered at me when I passed.

He said, "Have you come to play, or cause trouble, or both?"

He was trying to flirt.

"I came to meet a gentleman friend," I said.

"You're in the wrong joint," he said.

Bob thought he'd said something clever and smiled to himself. Stengel stood as I approached. He was late-retirement age. His eyes, set in his walnut head, were healthy enough to add up my assets. The obvious total was a well-rounded two.

"Ms. Sunday," he said. "Thank you for meeting with me."

He handed me the ends of his cold wax fingers to shake.

He added, "You won't regret it, I assure you."

I regretted it already, but I didn't want to damage his self-image by saying so. We sat down at the table, its top covered in gray Formica. I listened to his breathing attempts, waited for his equilibrium to readjust to the sitting position and for his stomach to settle.

When the time seemed right, I said, "Did you know Norman Parks very well?"

"I didn't know the Reverend Parks at all. I only heard him mentioned in connection with our work for the church."

Hearing Norm called Reverend startled my funny bone, but my snicker was irrelevant to grim Stengel.

He said, "The Reverend Parks and his unfortunate demise are of no concern to me. There would have been no reason for me to seek him out. I'm Jewish."

He was winded. I waited.

In his own good time he said, "In fact, there is very little that concerns me now. But I would like to set a few things in order before I leave this life. I need to clear my conscience. As you have no doubt noted, I am in ill health. Terminal, with a few months left, maybe."

He paused for a wheeze. Bob yelled at us, *did we want anything?* We didn't right now. Bob grumbled.

"I'm not going to my grave with this guilt weighing down on my head. As for my former partner, well, he'll have to remain behind and enjoy the consequences of his malfeasance."

"How bad is your guilt?"

"It doesn't get much worse. As for Reverend Parks, my guess is that he was, in the grand scheme of things, a minor nuisance who had to be dealt with."

I also remembered Norm in the same way, as a minor nuisance, but I resented Stengel saying it. Maybe he thought he had a right, since he was on the fast track to the finish line himself.

I said, "Why me? Why aren't you talking to the police instead?"

"You, my dear, don't understand how resilient and pervasive the web of corruption is. There are billions of dollars at stake. Money has power on it, and the more of it you have, the more power you've got."

"Thanks for the tip. If I ever come into a billion or so, I'll try to stay humble."

"You are aware, I'm sure, that the profits from marijuana are more than substantial in this province. And Brandish, you have met Brandish, haven't you? He controls a large portion of the trade, and he requires different methods to legitimize the proceeds. Millions of dollars of drug money per year, anonymous, of course, are donated to the church, and it finds its way back to the donors in the form of real estate, or payments for bogus services, or sent overseas to phony mission projects and into foreign bank accounts. Brandish is behind it all. And for a bonus, he uses religion as a front, so he can appear pious and project a righteous image to the public."

"And the authorities haven't been able to figure this out?"

"You don't understand. He's got his people in very high places."

"Let's play fill-in-the-blank. You need me in the equation because…?"

"I don't want my family to suffer for what I've done, and I don't want the small amount of time I have left taken from me by the police and any investigation they might undertake as a result of the information I am privy to."

He came up for air and then resubmerged.

He said, "In fact, if I were to go to the police, I would likely spend my last days in jail, or confined to a bed of their choosing. I'm confident—I did some checking on your level of competency—that you will be able to bring the facts to light and Brandish's criminal life to a satisfactory conclusion. I'm giving you the basic information, and you can take it from there."

"I'll admit I've been compared to Superwoman in the past, but my tights and magic lasso shrank in the wash. Besides, I was hired to find out who killed Norman, not destroy our province's economy."

"I believe you have more depth than that. There are records that still exist in Braithwaite's office that verify the facts I've been telling you. We will see if there is a way for you to get your hands on them."

"It sounds inviting, but I'm not sure that getting my hands on them is something I should be looking forward to. But while we're discussing facts, what's going on with the seniors' center at Whistler?"

"There was some trouble there. If my understanding of the situation is correct, Reverend Parks was getting greedy, and he made some threats. The project was never in danger. And it's recession-proof. I think your senior man at the church, Pastor Jessop, stuck his nose into the mix and got it a bit bloodied. If he gets foolish and tries to stop Brandish, I do believe he will be found to be in need of psychiatric care."

"He's not in good shape."

"You would think a man of his presumed understanding and experience would know better than to let the devil run his church."

"From what I've seen, it's not uncommon."

"Listen, little lady, if you're smart, you can use the information I provide in order to expose Brandish. How you do it is up to you, but there will be people who are receptive to uncovering the truth about his financial dealings. The number of deaths from the gang wars is becoming embarrassing. At the same time, Brandish has become too arrogant and too independent for his own good. The chamber of commerce isn't happy, and neither is the government. And the people who make crime their business aren't pleased with him either. The climate and timing are right for Brandish to be dethroned. He is not immune. He has powerful associates, but he also has some powerful enemies, in Asia and elsewhere, who would enjoy the opportunity to see him suffer and come toppling down."

"Let me see if I can summarize. You're telling me your dirty secrets because you figure clearing your conscience will lighten your load so you can float easier on your future heavenly cloud. And if I'm the one who exposes the dirt, then your family won't suffer any consequences. Forgive my candor, but it sounds to me like you've chosen me as an errand girl to deliver your revenge. Did they do you wrong, Mr. Stengel?"

"What difference does it make to you? You'll get what you want in the process. And for your information, since you have been so clever as to mention it, I don't believe in the existence of any heavenly cloud that I might be obliged to float on after I'm dead."

"I apologize. Then would you agree to a future rotting peacefully six feet under?"

Stengel expended some energy to wheeze at me.

I said, "One other thing, if you're telling the truth, why haven't we heard about any of this before now?"

"You are naive, my little lady."

"I might be naive, but I'm not your little lady."

Lechery died hard, and even though I felt some compassion for Mr. Stengel's terminal condition, I planned to skip his funeral. I'd had enough of him already. I also decided to forego lecturing him on taking responsibility for his life. His transgressions were killing him, but that was his business.

I said, "I'll think about your kind offer to help me in my journey."

"That's fine. See that you do," he said, and watched me rise. "We will be in touch, Ms. Sunday."

I said, "You might want to wait here for a few minutes before you leave. Brandish pinned a tail on me."

"You might have told me."

"I just did. What are you worrying about? He can't see us in this cellar."

"You're right. What's the use? It really doesn't matter to me now. I continue to forget my condition makes me immune to prosecution, but I'm sentenced to death nevertheless."

I appreciated Stengel's poetic bent. I wished he'd revealed it sooner. I might have formed a better opinion of him. It was too little too late. I granted him an understanding nod and then left him there to stew in his juices.

Bob sneered at me on my way out.

He said, "Maybe you'd like to make a donation to the cause for use of the office space?"

I ignored him, but I was happy he'd managed once again to express a complete thought.

* * *

It was time to visit Pastor Jessop again, while I was in the neighborhood. His house was a few blocks away. When I phoned, he said to come on over. Monday was his day off. I was there in fifteen minutes. The housekeeper escorted me to the lawn at the rear of the house. Pastor Jessop was lounging by the hole in his backyard. He wore his burgundy tracksuit and a black ball cap. His sunglasses looked like welder's goggles. He gestured for me to lie down beside him on a matching lounge chair. Propriety insisted I click myself up a few notches. He adjusted his attitude too.

The mouth below the black bug eyes said, "She always wanted a pool."

He pointed at the hole, and at what might have been, and then dismissed the aborted future with a backhanded wave.

"I don't see any reason to have one now," he said.

"No, why would you want to spoil your mudhole land-scaping?" I said.

The bug eyes under the hat weren't amused. I withheld my insight that he might be setting a bad Christian example for his neighbors.

"I didn't see you at the funeral," he said.

"I was doing my duty, having intimate fellowship with one of your eligible converts. At my age, you need to strike when the iron is hot. It might have been hotter, but Promise Keepers' promise number three intervened."

"Who's the fortunate man?"

I filtered his voice for sarcasm. He was sincere.

"Bert Smith," I said.

"You can't go wrong there."

Pastor Jessop looked up at the irritating sky.

"I've had enough of the sun," he said. "Let's go inside."

I waded after him through the shin-deep grass. It was in need of a cut. The rear of the house strangled in Virginia creeper, which competed with the ivy at the corners. Inside, his musty study rejected me, but I pushed through and found a chair. He tossed his ball cap and goggles onto his blotter, pulled his lamp's chain, and slumped behind his desk. His eyes were bloodshot.

"I met with your main man, Alec Brandish," I said.

"I see."

"Yes, I know you do. Why doesn't the church just come clean?"

"You know very well it's not that easy. It's funny how things happen."

"Yes, funny," I said.

I tried to appreciate how being the pastor of a criminal organization might help develop your sense of humor.

"I didn't pay that much attention to the books. Why would I? We had a very rich man running the business end. What a blessing, I thought."

Jessop was becoming detached and reflective. He didn't need me for anything.

He continued, "The congregation was growing in numbers and growing in the faith. We were a success. I didn't know what was going on at first, and by the time I did understand the scope of Brandish's deceit, it was too late. If I expose the corruption now, the faith of many will be destroyed in the process."

To remind him I was still in the room, I said, "Why don't you just tell the truth? Eventually it's going to come out."

Larry rediscovered me sitting there, jumped to his feet, and pointed his finger at my nose. He said, "Truth? What is truth? Truth didn't protect Cynthia. Do you think it was an accident? It was no accident. Her brakes failed, and that drunk got in the way. And he took the blame. It was all very convenient."

His point made, he fell back into his chair.

"I don't care about me," he said. His voice weakened. "June and I were meeting to see if we could do something… and then Norman, only a warning. And then Brandish promised me that…Amy…or Sally…if I go to the authorities, one of them will be next."

I didn't like the sound of that.

Sally hired me to protect Jessop, but there wasn't much I could do to protect him now, except try to prevent his plunge from being fatal when the bottom dropped out of his church. But maybe the church wouldn't fall, and business would carry on as usual. Who was going to stop it? Brandish's slime had oozed into the crevices of both church and state. There was no separation. Any attempt to clean up his sleaze promised to be as fruitful and pleasant as scrubbing a slug trail out of a shag rug. To counter the image, a fantasy floated into my mind, of brown eyes and strong arms, urging me to forget the world's schemes and Brandish's competent portrayal of the devil. Why bother? Take the easy way out.

"I'll need to examine my motives and priorities," I said. "This is beginning to get personal."

"He wouldn't hesitate if you were to cause him any grief," Jessop said.

"In that case, I'll have to buy some insurance."

"There's something else," Jessop said.

He picked up his goggles and faced the bulging lenses.

He said, "Brandish runs and controls the church board. But officially, and legally, I'm still the chairman."

"For a messenger of the Good News, you don't have much that's uplifting to report."

"Not anymore."

I left Pastor Jessop there to disintegrate. There wasn't a lot I could do about it.

* * *

CHAPTER NINE

Tuesday morning book club came early. I'd needed a diversion, though not a mindless one. We were in transition from *The Great Gatsby* to *The Shack*. *The Shack* was advertised as a Christian book, but it had been causing a lot of disturbance among the faithful. The secular world was eating it up. It was a best seller. My book club sisters were divided. Our leader Elsa rode the fence.

"I must admit it's quite a jump to take," Elsa said, "from *Gatsby* to *The Shack*, and we wouldn't even be doing *The Shack* if it wasn't so popular with the secular world."

"Do you think it is so popular with non-Christians because it degrades us?" Winnie said.

"What do you mean by degrades?" Elsa said.

"You know, believing in a God who is so human," Winnie said.

"That's the beauty of it," Lily said. "Anyone can relate. I know that it's depressing to begin with. I didn't want to carry on, but I forced myself to because it is so popular. There had to be something to it."

"Perhaps it would be helpful," Elsa said, "if we were to be more specific and attempt to examine the major themes in the book."

"I know one," Lily said. "God loves all of us. He loves everyone in the whole world."

"That's hardly unique as far as themes go," Elsa said.

Elsa was in a bullying mood this morning.

"But it is a theme," I said.

"But where's the Cross?" Winnie said. "I think the author is saying everyone gets there in the end. It's Universalist, and that's not Christian."

"You're not supposed to take it literally," Elsa said. "It's not theology. He wrote it for his kids, and then the whole thing got out of hand."

"Why is it so popular?" I said. "It's full of clichés, and there's no real story. It's mostly dialogue. I wondered when the bridge game was going to start."

"That's a little harsh," Elsa said. "But I suppose with your background…"

Elsa was on the attack this morning. The night sweats must have kept her awake again.

"What about my background?" I said.

I wasn't going to turn the other cheek. I'd been counting sheep too, but for other reasons.

Anne said, "Aren't you forgetting about Missy? That's the story."

"Child abduction, abuse, and murder are commonplace," I said.

My club mates didn't want to argue the point.

Lily, continuing on the love track, said, "I think it's popular because it portrays God like She's one of us. We can know Her, or Him like we can know anybody. And He wants us to know Her or Him. Actually, as we all know from reading it, there are two Hers and one Him, although one Her is called Papa. I think the author is suggesting that we can get to know Them without all the fuss."

"Heaven help us," Winnie said. "Do you mean that the Cross is the fuss?"

Our group shrugged, unwilling at this time to engage the question of dying to self.

Brave Anne said, "It's about forgiveness and healing. Mack discovers God is in control and that in the past he had wrong ideas about who God really is."

"Do you mean that's who God really is?" I said. "Aunt Jemima, a guy with a big nose, and an Asian chick? I can hardly wait for flapjack heaven."

"Your insights are racist and sexist, but at least you did read the book this time," Elsa said. She was trying to make up.

"There aren't any SparkNotes for it. But you're right about the racism. If I were African-American or Jewish, I'd wonder why God was a stereotype. But on the positive side, I did enjoy the acid trip near the end."

Elsa winced at me. If she wanted to be my girlfriend, she'd need to try harder.

Winnie said, "I don't know about acid trips, but to me the book is simply more fodder to feed those Emergent Church people who don't honor Scripture, the ones whose favorite expression is *it's all good*."

"Our church is a little like that now," Anne said. "It didn't used to be."

"I knew this would happen if we studied a Christian book," Elsa said, "even though some of us don't agree that it is a Christian book. We really should stick to the policy we agreed on so that we can avoid these controversies in the future. Thankfully, the books on our list for the rest of this year are secular."

"I think we should give the author the benefit of the doubt," Lily said. "There must be something good about it to have sold so many copies. Love is what the world needs more of, and if people, especially non-Christians, experience a more loving God in the book, a God they can relate to, then it's well worth it, even if there's a little theology in it that seems mixed up."

"Nicely summarized, Lily," Elsa said. "I think we should leave it at that. We don't need to carry on with it next week. We will simply go to the next selection, which is Steinbeck's *The Grapes of Wrath*. I know it's long, about six hundred pages, but I'm sure with commitment and perseverance, we can finish it by then. Perhaps some of us have already started it. I do apologize for this abrupt change of plans, but I think this is the best course given the circumstances. Are we all agreed?"

"The SparkNotes are way shorter," I said.

Elsa decided she didn't hear me.

Our club broke into small talk, and was in the process of adjourning early, when Lily got a call from her husband. He had some church news. Lily shared it with the rest of us. The police were holding one of our brothers in the faith for questioning in the murder of Norman Parks.

* * *

Back at the office I cranked on the Internet. Stan Sommers was their catch. The police weren't releasing any more details. I tapped an acquaintance of mine downtown for some more information on the case. She obliged and told me Stan had been seen near the Parks's home the day of the murder. His prison record and history of violence during his biker days, combined with the statement by Sally Parks that Stan had issued threats against Reverend Parks, resulted in his being taken into custody. I hoped he had a good lawyer. As for Sally, I had a few questions for her.

Pastor Jessop phoned. He'd heard the news too.

"It's impossible," he said. "It's just impossible."

Then there was silence. I sensed he was drifting away, searching for a desert island and a soft piece of sand to lie down on to lose himself counting coconuts. I paused to let my compassion leak out before I spoke.

"Not in this world it isn't," I said.

"Stan told me once that if I ever needed anything…but that was quite a long time ago. And I only mentioned in passing the minor trouble I was having with Norman. It's impossible. He wouldn't do anything like that, especially if it also helped Brandish. Stan hated him for staying clean and above the law, while the little people like him served their time in jail."

"Stan worked for Brandish?"

"It was years ago. He wouldn't work for Brandish again, not after going to jail, would he? Stan reformed. There's no chance he killed Norman for Brandish."

"Would you prefer that he did it for you?"

"What?"

"Forgive me, I've laughed at funerals before too."

"He didn't do it at all, don't you see? It's a setup. Brandish is behind it. They'll discover evidence soon that clears Stan, and then they won't have any more suspects, and the case will go cold, and then everyone will forget about Norman."

"Why would Sally try to implicate Stan?"

"She did what?"

"Sally told police that Stan issued threats against Norman. Stan told Norman to stay away from you, or else."

"That's ridiculous. He wouldn't do that, and Sally would never say that to the police. I'll ask her what really happened."

"Where would you like to go from here?"

"I'm not going to go anywhere from here. And why are you asking me? My daughter hired you. Ask her where she wants to take this. I'm done. I've had enough. Whatever happens, I'm not going to try to stop it."

"You are the only one who can make something positive come out of all this."

"We've been through that. No one else is going to get hurt because of me. If you want to play God, go ahead. That's up to you."

"I would, but I failed omniscience."

"If I were you, I would talk about it with your new friend Bert and then decide what you're going to do."

"You're right, men always know best."

Jessop grumbled and then said, "Suit yourself," before hanging up.

My self-image had been more godlike before I talked to Jessop. Now I was insecure. I tried to stop the thought, to push it out—it didn't belong in my brain—but it pushed its way in, and there it was. Why did he have to bring Bert into it? I shoved back. Bert's interest in me was genuine. I'd felt the spark when we met. I trusted him. The only investigating of him I was going to do would be of the personal kind. End of story. And if I had to be a fool, I was going to do it the right way and be a fool for love. I didn't have anything better planned for the rest of my life anyway.

As for Sally, we had some catching up to do. She answered the phone wearing a hushed religious voice that sounded like a princess granting the lower classes an extra crust of bread for Christmas. She'd put it on for my benefit. I advised her to stick her head under a cold shower and then look forward to modeling a new, improved attitude for me when I arrived.

Otherwise, she might expect a scene. She understood my meaning.

I examined my own attitude on the way over and decided it needed to change. Sally was challenged enough without my anger giving her one more reason not to engage reality. The closer I got to her house, the slower my heart thumped. It was preparing to beat to her sad tune. But I still wanted to know why she'd kept former biker Stan's threats from me. And had she hidden any other minor details? There was an outside chance Stan had done the deed, but a paddle was a sloppy hit for a man of his caliber, unless emotions had gotten into it.

She let me in and retreated to her exercise room. I followed her. She wore a pink jogging suit and pink headband. She mounted her elliptical trainer and began to move in earnest. She was either working out her grief or getting in shape for the next guy. I sat sidesaddle on the weight bench and waited to see when she'd start to sweat.

I said, "If I'd known, I would have brought my jogging outfit and water bottle."

"Is that how you stay in such good shape?"

She was flattering me. I didn't mind.

"No, I do Pilates a couple of times a year. So let's hear it. Why didn't you tell me about Stan?"

She was moving her pleasingly plump assets like she thought she was going somewhere.

She said, "To protect my father, of course, not to cause him any more grief."

"I'm working for you, remember? We're not supposed to have any secrets."

"I apologize. I'm not accustomed to being investigated by the police, or hiring a private detective, or having my husband murdered. If I have behaved badly in your eyes, I'm sorry."

She'd spat her list of jerky excuses at me in a hissy fit, but she wasn't winded, or sorry.

"I forgive you. Now let's go on to the next part of our quiz. How much do you know about Norman's involvement with Alec Brandish?"

"I don't see any reason not to tell you the truth."

I was happy about that, since her honesty was so selective.

She said, "When I saw their relationship develop, you know, the way they got along, I began to think they were gay, but then I discovered their little secret. They were only buddies, and Brandish was providing Norman with women."

I tried to imagine Brandish having a buddy, or Norm having one, for that matter. After a few seconds, I gave up.

"Then why did you want your husband to take over running the church, when you knew the spiritual condition he was in?"

She swung to a halt and dismounted. "I have explained this to you before. I wanted Dad out, period. He wasn't going to be the one who took the blame for what has happened to the church, and Norman was already corrupted, so why not let him and Brandish take over, as long as Dad was out of it? My dad is an honest man, you know. You should have seen him when he was younger. Mom and Dad were a force for good in this city. And since you have concluded he wasn't having an affair with June either, that gives him a clean slate."

Her point made, she sprang aboard and resumed speed. I tried to see Jessop her way. It was hard to do. He'd allowed Brandish to take over, and now, after riding the glory trail for years, thanks to Brandish, he was too old and exhausted to do anything about the state of his church. And as for Sally's performance, she was showing her resilience. There had to be more guts in those romance novels than I thought, or maybe her delusion was total, and she'd become her own heroine consumed by victimhood, her future hanging on the hope of a hunk striding into her life to double up on the back of her trainer.

"Do you remember Toronto?" I said.

"No, I was just a baby then. Why do you ask? And what do you know about Toronto?"

"I just wondered. You said your dad was different when he was younger."

"I see. Well, I was only born in Toronto, and Amy too, but we grew up here, in Vancouver. Is that really why you came over, to ask me about my childhood?"

I saw no reason to introduce the question of whether she'd grown up or not. Who was I to judge?

"How much do you know about Brandish and the church finances?"

"Only what I've read between the lines. Norman was expecting a huge raise when he took over. At least that's what he was asking for. He said the church could afford it, considering its yearly revenue."

"I've seen last year's balance sheet, and there seems to be too much income for the size of the congregation. And I've discovered there's a large amount of money that comes in anonymously, and that means there are no charitable donation receipts issued for it. What could explain that?"

"I'm not an accountant. People give. That's all I know."

Sally's face wasn't dripping, but it was moist. She knew more about the money subject than she wanted me to know.

"Do you think Stan murdered your husband?"

Sally paused and then decided she'd had enough. She stepped down, took her towel, and dabbed her white face and pink cheeks and pretended to think deep thoughts on the subject.

"Stan loved my dad. He saved Stan's life. Stan might have done it."

"So tell me the truth. Who do you really think did it?"

"I won't lie to you. Brandish was unhappy with Norman for something he did. Whatever it was, I know Norman wasn't going to back down. And I do know that Mr. Brandish is not a very nice man. The difficult part is how you're going to prove he did it."

Sally was aware of the challenges ahead. She didn't expect that anyone, including me, was going to prove anything against Brandish. She knew I wasn't going to be able to protect her father, either. She knew that. She lied to me and hired me. She must have had a reason.

"If Brandish goes down, so does the church and your dad," I said.

"Well then, that just can't be allowed to happen, can it? One of the other pastors, one who isn't corrupted by Brandish, will take over the church, and my dad can retire in peace."

I said, "What's stopping Brandish from installing one of his flunky pastors in the top job?"

"It's out of our hands," she said. "But I'm glad you finally realized it was Brandish and not my father."

"I'll mail you your bill."

"I see. Well, I imagine our relationship has ended."

"Don't cry your eyes out after I'm gone."

"As I said, I'm sorry. Life must go on."

That was debatable, but I wasn't in the mood to engage her on the subject. I slipped off the bench, raised an eyebrow at her life, and then left her there to cool down.

* * *

CHAPTER TEN

It was Bert night again. We had a date to play pool. He wanted to learn, and I wanted to teach him. I discovered on the way to Benny's Pool Room that I'd lost my tail, and there was no way I wanted to find him. Brandish must have concluded I was a defeated detective. That conclusion seemed right. There were a few tables occupied when we arrived. Slow Bob was happy to see us when he realized that tonight I was a paying customer. He gave us the balls. I didn't want Bert to be any more embarrassed than he had to be, so I steered us to a back table. I'd even left my cue at home. I'd use one from Slow Bob's warped collection on the rack. And as a courtesy, I'd buttoned my blouse to the top so I wouldn't draw attention from the boys in the room and throw them and us off our game. I'd have preferred a better view for Bert, but he was the kind of guy who had the capacity to appreciate modesty; he'd rejected his former depraved self and set his sights on being pure. I was fine either way. We decided to play nine-ball. I racked them, and Bert tried to break. I could see it was going to be a long game. He looked way better than he shot. I would have to go easy on the throttle to keep our competition from looking ridiculous. I was holding the power, but I wasn't sure I liked it that way. To fake making an effort, I knocked down the one ball, and the two, and then let up on the three.

Bert was admiring my style. He said, "You hold that cue like you spent your life in a pool hall."

"My dad did, and he took me along most of the time. Would you like me to show you how to hold yours?"

"I don't mind if you do."

I showed him how to make a proper bridge with his left hand, and how to stroke with his right, and how to stand for proper balance. Then he took a chop at the cue ball and hit the three. I loved his style, not with the cue, but the way he leaned over the table. He was a natural. Even though he was a hacker at pool, I hoped he was a straight shooter in every other way. He straightened up to see if I was impressed. I was.

"Nice shot," I said. "You're getting the feel of it already, in only one short lesson."

"I've got a good teacher. I wouldn't mind if you taught me to play like this all night."

Before we got ahead of ourselves, I said, "Pastor Jessop suggested I ask your advice about something."

"What was *his* advice?"

Bert had exchanged his fun companion outfit for his lawyer's uniform in one easy question. I knocked in the three ball to change the subject, and then the four. I left the five over the side pocket for Bert. He remembered my instructions and took his time. His rhythm was improving. He sank the ball, and we both cheered.

The boys a few tables away projected a collective sneer in our direction. One of them mumbled, "Oh, come on, give us a break."

My feelings weren't a bit hurt.

"I need to decide if it's worth it," I said.

Bert, overextending himself instead of using the rest, miscued on the six. Disappointed in his performance, he said, "You mean you have encountered complications concerning Norman's death."

"I'll show you how to use the ladies' aid next time," I said.

I pocketed the six in the top left corner and missed the seven in the right side, not on purpose, but my expletive was silent. I'd left my naughty mouth back in Toronto, and it hadn't found its way west, yet.

I said, "There's a lot at stake. It's not just about Norman; it's about Pastor Jessop, and Alec Brandish, and the whole church. And then there's Amy and Sally. More people could lose their lives."

Bert had a long shot on the seven. He added some macho to his stroke and missed. He shook his head at the wayward ball and said, "Do you have some personal interest in the outcome?"

"Maybe, but officially I'm out of it. Norman hired me to do a little investigating for him. And then after Norman was killed, Sally hired me. But I've been fired. To be more accurate, I quit."

"So we'll be able to spend more time together, then?"

I knocked in the seven and the eight but played bad position on the nine. My bank in the side went astray, and the cue ball came around to give Bert an easy shot in the right corner to finish the game.

"You can do it," I said.

He lined up the shot and said, "What are we playing for?"

"I don't gamble anymore. It's a fool's game."

He stroked the cue ball, and the nine rolled in.

"Nice shot, you win," I said.

Bert came over and gave me a consolation squeeze.

He said, "Do you always let your opponents win?"

"No, never, you beat me fair and square."

I squeezed him back. The boys in the room were disgusted, but Slow Bob, leaning on the counter, his chin cupped in one hand, was grinning at a fantasy of some kind playing in his mind. We shot a few more games. I let Bert win the last one. Slow Bob returned from his reverie in time to collect for the table and thank us for our patronage. Then we left Benny's to pursue our next adventure in courting.

We climbed into my Hummer and headed back down Broadway. I'd picked up Bert earlier to see how he'd enjoy riding shotgun. He took it like a man. I drove down to Spanish Banks. I had an urge to be a teenager again. I found us a stall to park our passion. The fall night was clear, perfect weather to watch the submarine races through the steamy windshield.

"Thanks for being a gentleman about losing," I said.

"I feel like a winner."

Bert made his move to get us more comfortable.

"What would you do?" I said.

"I'm doing it."

"No, I mean about the case, and Pastor Jessop, and the church?"

"You said there was a lot at stake. But what's your interest in it now that you're no longer being retained?"

"There is the matter of justice."

"Justice, what's that?"

"I thought you worked in the attorney general's office?"

"Like I said, what's justice? You might consider letting the police take care of the investigation. I know you're more than capable, but you might be out of your league with Brandish. He's a lot to handle."

I pulled back from Bert. I didn't like the sound of that.

"How well are you acquainted with Brandish?"

"He's not a person to argue with. I wouldn't like to see anything happen to you."

We agreed on that. I pulled farther away. It was dark, but I saw two Berts. One was illusion, the other reality. But I didn't know which was which. I was too confused to carry on. A headache was the answer. I turned the ignition key. Bert knew what was going on, or he didn't.

I said, "I just remembered I forgot to put the cat out, and the pain in my head is starting to rap."

"That was sudden," Bert said.

"You know women."

I drove Bert to his building on Georgia. On the way he didn't bother me with any conciliatory small talk, which was a brownie point in his favor. When we arrived, he said, "Would you like to come in?"

I said, "No, I wouldn't want to jeopardize your Promise Keepers record."

Bert let himself out. He said, "I'll call you tomorrow to see how you're feeling."

"I'm going to survive."

I left him there holding the moment. My headache was gone. I drove justice home, my new companion, riding in the passenger seat. Brandish was slop that needed flushing. I saw my happy face pulling the lever. He deserved to go down for Jessop's wife alone, not to mention for all the others he had corrupted, or erased, on his waddling journey. But I knew if I lost the game, I'd miss out on the thrill of consummating solitary middle age and hunching onward into osteoporosis. If I won, and Brandish was jailed for a very long time, I was still a loser, unless dear Bert was in fact true blue and not one of the syndicate servers. If he was the real deal, I would be living on Rapture Street forevermore. And I would have to remember to buy a cat.

The next day came early. Amy was on my cell, wishing for an audience. I agreed to meet her at my office at nine. I endured the lineup at the Tim Horton's drive-through and juggled a black extra large on the way to jerking my system awake. The princess was late to arrive. I waited and took in the news online. The world was coming apart, as usual. I surfed forward to winter fashions and was discovering *ten secrets to a life of happiness* when Amy made her entrance. She was the same, her cute, sassy face all in a pucker over life.

"You're late," I said.

She hadn't noticed and was in no mood to discuss it.

"I'm told you have ceased being employed by my sister."

She was trying on for size a performance of *being in no mood to be trifled with*. I considered cowering to encourage her, but decided my compliance would only contribute to her negative growth.

"Who told you, a little birdie?" I said.

Her dramatic assault a failure, she collapsed into my client's chair.

"I've changed my mind about pressuring Braithwaite," she said. "I think my dad is going to escape and retire without being disgraced. That's the way it's going to go. There's nothing anyone can do about Brandish."

"I thought you didn't like the way church is. Have you lost your hope for reformation?"

"There's nothing anyone can do. It is what it is."

"What about Norman? Do we just forget about him?"

"You know as well as I do they have a suspect. The police arrested Stan Sommers, one of my dad's converts."

"He didn't do it."

"You will never expose Brandish."

"If that's the only reason you came, you could have phoned it in."

"I didn't want to miss the warmth of your presence."

"Don't you think it's kind of neat and tidy the way Norman was taken out of the way? Now your dad is free to retire without any scandal tagging along to ruin the foursome at the country club."

"He doesn't play golf."

"Just to keep you abreast of the news, I had considered dropping the whole twisted business, since I'm no longer on your sister's payroll. But now I'm all alone in the world again, and I don't have much of anything else to keep me out of the pool room. So I thought I would sniff around some more and maybe leave a trail myself. Who knows what I might dig up?"

"Oh, so sad, your new boyfriend let you down. I'm sorry to hear that. They're not to be trusted. That's been my experience."

"Trust is a big issue," I said. "Your dad learned that the hard way."

"I hope your digging around in the muck doesn't smear my dad. And I wouldn't want to see anything bad happen to you either, even though you do have glaring character defects that annoy me."

"I've already had bad things happen to me. And, as I've suggested to you before, why don't you get to the heart of the matter and straighten yourself out? You don't really want to waste your life pretending, do you?"

"No, Mother, you've got me there. I'll go right out and engage the future and change my life around just for you."

"I'd prefer you did it for yourself, but if you need my assistance, I'd be happy to be your inspiration."

"You won't change your mind about your mission, I suppose?"

"I'm touched. But if anything happens to me, I've left you my attitude in the will."

"It's not something I would cherish."

"Have you got a job yet?"

"If you have to know, I'm interviewing for a production assistant's position this afternoon."

She elevated her nose an inch, proud of her accomplishment. Then she decided our time together was ended.

"Good-bye," she said.

She sprang from the chair, turned tail, and slammed my door on the way out.

"Good-bye," I said.

I was left there to harden. No more Ms. Nice Gal. Jessop had cursed his own destiny. He sowed, and he was going to reap. Sentimentality and justice slept in separate beds. Something had to be done, and there was nothing else to do but test Braithwaite's nerve. Stengel said the evidence could be had, and Braithwaite had it. Before I began my assault, my cell rang the Bert song. I faced the music. He wanted to know how I was today. He discovered how I was when I wasn't interested in telling him. He desired we meet to discuss our issues. I said playing the hot twosome was out of the question until I checked the wisdom of that course of action with my pastor. He said at least I hadn't lost my sense of humor. I said it was always the last to go, and beeped him off.

I thought about stalling by taking another tour of the day's news events on the Internet, followed by a few games of FreeCell. But I was too mad for that. I rang Braithwaite's office, and he took my call. I was so surprised to hear his voice answer, I forgot what I was supposed to say next.

"You talked to Stengel?" he said.

He was helping me. That was a switch. I suspected he was sitting there pulling on his mustache and looking pensive.

"Your ex-partner's a nice fellow. I enjoyed his breathing on me."

"He mentioned to you some information, which I might be able to let you have as long as a certain party isn't apprised of the source."

"In case you haven't thought this through, aren't you concerned you might incriminate yourself?"

"You needn't expend your energy worrying on my account. Special precautions have been taken to eliminate the possibility that I will be held accountable for any wrongdoing."

"And what do you expect me to do with the information?"

"I understand you have a friend who works in the attorney general's office. Perhaps he would agree to be of assistance."

"You're a big boy. Why don't you give it to him yourself? You see him in church every Sunday."

"As you no doubt are aware, keeping a safe distance from the law is most desirable in a situation such as this."

"Why do you want to blow the whistle on Brandish? He keeps you well stocked in pencils, doesn't he?"

"Let us simply say that there are other interests I have pertaining to this whole matter, which are bound to bring greater satisfaction to me personally as long as there are no complications that might hinder my future prospects."

"Okay, you've sold me on your sincerity. When and how are you going to grace me with this information?"

"We will make it simple for you. The package will arrive at your office this afternoon. A friend of yours will make the delivery. And thank you, Ms. Sunday, for calling. I trust our business is concluded for today."

"You trust right. Good day, Mr. Braithwaite."

Braithwaite sounded pleased, like a rat chortling over his cheese. I was being set up, but why? It was clear now that Stengel had been the talent scout, measuring my range for a role they'd written. And now they were sending me the script. Whatever they were planning, I hoped I wouldn't trip over the furniture. They were still working as a team. Maybe they'd circulated the rumors themselves that their split was acrimonious, as a cover for future endeavors that Stengel's family might profit from. Either way, Stengel's eviction from his body was imminent. And he was investing some of his precious remaining Earth time to play along, even though the thrill had to be gone. And now they'd dragged my estranged pal Bert into it. I was still willing to go the whole route with Bert, if he was clean. Fear of living the journey alone made fools of us all.

I had an urge to take a stroll before the evidence arrived. I rang Bert back; he was thrilled to go for a walk. I met him on Granville Island, where the tourists and the sun hadn't been told summer was over. I coaxed him out of his sheepish grin by taking his arm and telling him how neat he looked in his blue work suit.

He responded to my peace initiative by exclaiming, "Justice for all."

I received his calculated charm as a good start and forgot we had a war going on. We warmed up to our slow walk, the connection opening, sparks flashing. We both smiled in passing at the tempting Granville Island Hotel, and then at each other, but it wasn't on today's to-do list for either of us. I turned for another look and then remembered Lot's wife. I was happy that pillars of salt were no longer God's style and sad that Bert continued firm in his forward motion. The conflict excited me. Bert's presence had again nullified the PI in me, and that was dangerous, which also excited me. I was now tired of the walk, the view, the ocean chop, and the pretty white boats. We found a table outside a café and ordered our lunch. Bert said he owned a boat, docked at Horseshoe Bay, and all I had to do was give him the nod and he'd take me. I said I'd make a decision on going for a bounce on the waves if there was anything left to bounce after the justice deed was done. Since the subject had now come up, it was time to spoil our day.

"I'm getting the evidence on Brandish this afternoon. Are you willing to take it to your leader?"

"Why doesn't your source take it, and why are you involved?"

"Whistle-blowers work in mysterious ways."

"It won't help my career."

"You'd make a great crusader."

"Crusaders die lonely. The system is amoral. We all serve the bottom line, and the bottom line lacks the capacity to care."

"I thought you were shallower than that. So you're not just another handsome face."

"I love you. I think you know that. And that's the only reason why I would consider it."

I wasn't sure why he had chosen now to threaten me. He'd gutted my fantasy, handed me the reality, and numbed my tongue. He saw me freeze, and his compassion, coming to my aid, said, "When will you have the information?"

The love words would have come out if he'd given me more time. My emotions tried again, but then my mind interfered and answered his question.

"I...uhh...this afternoon," I said.

"You know you're stronger than I am."

"I'd love for you to take over. I could use the rest."

"I'd love it too," he said, "but you wouldn't like some of my decisions."

"I wasn't asking you to lord it over me."

"We can share the position," he said.

"I'll look forward to exploring our positions after Brandish is fitted for his striped prison tent."

"Do you want me to pick up the documents?" he said.

"I'll bring them tonight, if you want to get together."

"I would like to get together permanently."

"Let's cool down until the job's done."

I was surprised by my mature approach to happiness, and a little proud.

"I don't mind waiting. We have the rest of our lives to be together."

I liked the sound of that and silenced my suspicion of Bert's motives with the assurance life didn't have to be a recurring bad habit. I loved Bert, or the idea of having someone like him. The idea itself was my protection. If he was counterfeit, I'd drop him and transfer the idea to someone else. If he was genuine, I would have a real person to splice with. We finished lunch, Bert paid, and we walked back the way we came, the defiant sun burning up there, warm and glowing, his arm around my shoulder, mine around his waist, middle-aged lovers holding on, resisting the coming autumn.

I waited in my office for the package to arrive. I was surprised to see Stengel wheeze through my door, carrying a bundle under his arm. He tottered in, his eyes desperate to stay open and alive.

"This is it," he said, and pressed his treasure onto my desk. "This will put him away for life."

He emphasized the word *life*, like it was precious to him.

He said, "These are the actual records of the money transactions. Take good care of them. They are the only ones that exist. The electronic files have been deleted." Then he added, in his best effort at being in a hurry, "I can't stay."

"That's too bad," I said. "We could go through the records together and share a trip down Memory Lane."

"As pleasant a prospect as that is, Ms. Sunday, I'm afraid I must be going. I don't want to shorten my life any further."

I wasn't sure if he meant the excitement of my company might do him in, or it was dangerous for him to stay.

"I understand. Don't let me keep you."

"I know you will be sure to get that into the right hands. Until we meet again, Ms. Sunday."

Stengel took his leave in under two minutes. I was left with the bundle and a death scent for air freshener. I cranked open a window. The brown paper package was tied with twine, a nice touch. Stengel, disguised as the local butcher, had delivered the bottom line. I cut the twine and found several folders inside labeled: Church Accounts. I took the tour. Stengel hadn't told a lie. There was enough evidence linking Brandish to money laundering and illegal transfers of funds to keep him sweating regrets in the prison laundry room till hell dissolved his floor. Pastor Jessop had some bad times coming too, but he'd danced with the devil and must have known that a careless slew foot was bound to scuff his shoes. I'd been listening to the siren outside increase its wail as I was going through the church finances. Now it had stopped below my window. I took the elevator down. Stengel lay on the lobby floor, the paramedics tending to their business. There was no sign of foul play, unless you counted his life. They covered him with the sheet and wheeled him out of the building faster than he'd entered. No siren accompanied his departure. I buried the putrid thought of stirring up some grief for Stengel. It would be a waste of energy. He'd coughed up his life with eyes wide open, and I had better things to do. Across the street a gray sedan pulled away from the curb. I guessed my turn was coming, but not quite yet.

* * *

CHAPTER ELEVEN

I rode the elevator back up to my office, where I lay my dizzy head on the desk. But it wasn't spinning from the elevator ride. The gray sedan had begun to get to me, and my stomach was harmonizing with my head in a fear duet. I lowered the volume by thinking simple, logical thoughts. They'd helped Stengel die, but didn't prevent delivery of the evidence. They'd killed the messenger, but didn't care if the message was delivered. There was something wrong with that. I was floating facedown in my pool of misgivings when Pastor Jessop called to say he wanted to meet with me, along with Amy and Sally. I told him, if it was something he had to do, I wasn't going to stay home and spoil his party. He said he'd made a major decision, and he thought we should all talk about it. I didn't ask him why I merited inclusion in his family's business, but I guessed that my goading him to fall on his sword was the reason. He was planning to wipe the scorn off my face in person. Since he'd told me about Brandish's threats directed at Sally and Amy, I hadn't been as thrilled to see him come forward and confess, but now that I had the financial records, Brandish would have to swivel his head in my direction instead. Jessop invited me to meet him and the girls at the scene of the crime, at Sally's, the next morning at ten. My news about Stengel disturbed him the way that kind of news is supposed to. He said he was sorry to hear that, but he himself had never met the man. And we left it at that.

My head revisited the desk blotter, my mind searching the pool for Bert. He was down there, inviting me to dive deeper. When I noticed he was naked, I surfaced. I wasn't in the mood. Stengel was gone. Life was hard, but I didn't want to go next. I could take the files to the police or follow Braithwaite's instruction and give them to Bert. Bert was safer, and if he did me wrong, then I would know that the sweet words and flowers were for show, while his heart belonged to another. I phoned to arrange our business date. He must have left his chastity pledge in his other suit, because he panted back at me. I got in the mood. Our chemistry felt good, but I knew bad things were about to happen when my brain shifted into neutral. My father taught me that. Bert was coming to get me at six thirty. I had the package to give him, but for now I would postpone giving him my life.

Bert arrived on time. He'd put his gentleman outfit back on; his tongue had retracted. He saw the package and nodded when I slid into his Beemer. We were off to the movies to see *The Little Traitor*. I hoped the title wasn't prophetic. After we parked, I checked the street for the gray sedan. He must have been on his dinner break. Bert took the bundle and locked it in the trunk. My heart waved it good-bye; my stomach fluttered a butterfly. We tried to snuggle in the show, but the package had already come between us. Each of us had a reason to squirm. I knew my reason but didn't know his. For me, the transaction had been too easy. For Bert, he was either uncomfortable being the middleman or he was finished with the job and it was time for moving on. *The Little Traitor* ended. Hearts burst, and tears flowed. Bert and I were troubled. We had our own story to work out. I was hoping that when we came to the end, we'd discover ours had been a comedy. On the way home, there was no talk of after-show snacks or coffee or stopping to park. We rode in unsettled silence. In the side mirror, I noticed the gray sedan following us. Bert saw it too.

"Our friend is back," I said. "He was there this afternoon when Stengel breathed his last."

"Stengel the accountant? You mean he's dead?"

"He was a sick man."

"I'll take you home."

"Are you planning to go home alone with the evidence?" I said.

"I see your point. Maybe I'll come in, if I'm invited."

"As long as you don't tell the attorney general I'm easy."

"There's nothing easy about you."

Bert found a guest parking spot at my town house and retrieved the package from the trunk. We didn't take the time to hold hands on the way in. Once inside, we bolted the door. The gray sedan parked itself across the street. The package that had separated us earlier was now pulling us together in the excitement. I remembered I had to be a lady and not take advantage of him.

I said, "It's probably a good idea if you stay here tonight."

Bert faked wobbly knees and grabbed hold of me. He said, "I'm willing, but the flesh is weak."

I got the message. He was straying from his commitment to the straight and narrow, but there was no room for him in my room tonight.

"Don't worry, my flesh is strong enough for both of us. Tonight we're sleeping in separate rooms."

Bert pulled back.

He said, "I'm beginning to have doubts about our future together. Will it always be like this?"

"You mean my job or the sleeping arrangements?"

"Sometimes we're so close we seem like one person, and other times it's like we're strangers."

He sounded like a woman. I was having my doubts too.

"Welcome to real life. What were you doing with all those other women, playing make-believe?"

"We were mostly having a good time."

"That's what I thought."

I pulled a blanket and a pillow out of the closet and tossed them at the couch. Bert pretended to sulk. I was too tired to enjoy his act. He found the clicker and soothed himself with TSN.

"Try to keep it down," I said. "And don't bother coming in to kiss me goodnight."

I went to my room realizing we'd fallen from breathing sweet fire to impersonating the dull and the weary. I had an excuse. I was waiting till tomorrow to see who he was. Was he Bert the beautiful or Bert the same as all the others? Right now the gray sedan didn't concern me as much as the answer to that.

We both slept like we were normal. There were no bumps in the night. In the morning the gray sedan was gone, or in hiding. Coffee was for breakfast. Bert gulped his, pecked me on the cheek, and escaped. The honeymoon was over. He was going straight to the office with the evidence, or that's what he said. I had a date with Jessop and his girls.

I took the trip up the mountain to Sally's house. It wasn't raining. The sun was focused on burning the clouds off. Nature looked as stunning as always. But like too much of anything, beauty held the potential to arouse ultimate boredom. I called Bert. He was at his office with the package. He was busy and forgot to ask me what I was doing tonight and had to go. I didn't want to read much into that, but told the driver in front of me that he was a bad driver and a bad person. My Toronto mouth had made itself heard. I was just as happy that I was the only one around to hear it. I looked forward to my morning meeting with the Jessops, but didn't like what I saw. No matter what Jessop had decided to announce, my news flash was going to place me at the center of attention, even though that wouldn't be fair to the others. But I'd never made much of an effort to be well liked. Sally met me at the door, as was her habit, and escorted me into her life of white, where Amy and Jessop waited. Jessop was standing, looking out at the pool, and didn't acknowledge my entrance. Amy was sitting in my favorite chair. She riffled through *Christian Romance Magazine* for my benefit and faked a smile at me. I returned her greeting in kind and found a lesser chair to sit in.

"Jane's here," Sally said to her dad.

Jessop, his death muse interrupted, turned and nodded and then joined daughter Sally on the white leather couch. I noticed they were shoeless. It must have been a family tradition they reverted to when they got together. They tried not to notice my spikes, except for Amy, who was turning up her nose.

"I'm glad you came," Jessop said to me. "This hasn't been easy, and I want to thank you for helping me see the situation more clearly. Don't worry, I'm not planning to launch into a sermon on righteousness. I'm not qualified for that anymore. I simply want to tell you and the girls that I'm going to go to the police and confess to my crime, which is something I should have done a long time ago. There have been financial irregularities that I have turned my back on. But no more. The truth is going to come out."

Jessop was the sanest I'd ever seen him. Truth must have jerked him down from hysteria heaven.

"Don't do it, Dad," Sally said. "Then it would have all been for nothing."

We looked at Sally and wanted to know what she meant by *all*.

She said, "I mean your career, all you've done and sacrificed over the years. Why not let Brandish carry on? The church can have a new pastor, and you can be out of it. You can retire with honor."

"What's retirement now? Your mother's gone. My reputation isn't worth anything…It has all been false. God's justice is going to prevail."

"What did God ever do for you?" Amy said.

"He gave me you, for one," Jessop said, "and your sister, and your mother, and the opportunity to have a fruitful ministry. I was the one who destroyed it. It was my pride. I had to have the biggest and the best in town. But I let Brandish give it to me. Who knows what would have happened if I had done it God's way?"

"We will all be ruined," Sally said. "Have you thought of that?"

"Come on, Sally, let's get real," Amy said. "Nobody cares about us, one way or the other. It's Dad who's going to suffer for this, not us."

"So, you're satisfied with his decision?" Sally said. "You're happy to let him go to jail."

"It's not my decision, or yours," Amy said, and to me she said, "You're awfully quiet this morning. Don't you have something clever to say?"

"I'm glad your dad has decided to go to the police. It makes my job easier."

"What is your job?" Amy said, "I thought you quit."

"I saw the light too."

"What does that mean?" Amy said. "You failed to protect my dad, and you don't have a clue who killed Norman. And now it seems like you're telling us you've had a sudden revelation."

I said, "Braithwaite and Stengel coughed up the books. The Crown Prosecutor's office should have them by now. Brandish is going to answer for his crimes."

Jessop digested my revelation. And then he laughed. Sally and Amy looked at their dad but didn't even manage a chuckle.

"That doesn't help us at all," Sally said. "Dad is still going to be exposed, and we might all go to jail."

"What are you talking about?" Amy said. "We haven't done anything wrong."

"You're right," Sally said. "They can't prove I knew anything about it, especially with my poor Norman gone."

"They'll never get Brandish," Jessop said. "He's got too many friends in high places. Besides, I'm responsible. I signed everything he put in front of me, no questions asked."

"What about the church?" Amy said. "It's going to be destroyed in the scandal."

"I'm surprised you care," I said. "I thought you told me, *it is what it is.*"

Jessop said, "She means there are a lot of honest, sincere people who are going to be devastated by this. The church is going to disintegrate, and some are going to have their faith destroyed. That's why I had a lot of soul-searching to do before I made my decision to confess. Of course, that's irrelevant now."

"It's not worth it," Sally said, "just to get Brandish punished. The police aren't suspecting him of killing Norman. Maybe that biker did do it after all."

Sally had changed her story again. I'd noticed she constructed reality to suit herself, as she went along, depending on the audience. The trick was to know when she was lying to us.

"Detective Jane doesn't think he did it," Amy said.

"Well maybe Brandish hired him to do it," Sally said. "Have you considered that?"

Jessop said, "Stan wouldn't kill Norman. He left that life behind when he was converted."

"People backslide," Sally said. "Have you considered that he might have done it for you, because Norman was trying to get rid of you?"

We were all surprised by Sally's candor. Amy glanced down at *Christian Romance Magazine* on the coffee table and then up at me. I had nothing to say.

Jessop came to Sally's rescue and said, "Stan knew I wasn't worried about that. We talked often. And while we're on the subject, why did you say he threatened Norman?"

"He did threaten Norman," Sally said. "I heard him on the phone. Norman told me too…my poor Norman."

Jessop and Amy's faces shot blanks. Their sympathy for Sally had dried up. Mine had evaporated days ago.

"Never mind," Jessop said, "there's a good chance Norman's killer will be found when Brandish's activities are exposed."

"And that means they'll arrest you too," Amy said, and she began to cry.

Sally followed suit for something appropriate to do. I had none to spill, but I hoped at least that when Blind Justice made her ruling, she lifted her blindfold long enough to wink at Pastor Jessop.

"I hope you're satisfied," Amy said to me.

"Don't blame her," Jessop said. "Jane has done me a favor. With the church's books in the hands of the prosecutor's office, I won't have to point any fingers, except at myself."

"I've got a feeling the church is going to lose its charity status," I said.

"You *are* a genius," Amy said.

"There will be a mass exodus," Jessop said. I skipped pointing out his accidental pun, but daughter Amy rolled her eyes. "But there's nothing I can do about that," he said. "Besides, they will be better off elsewhere."

"I'm willing to be a character witness for you," I said, "and testify that you decided to come forward before you knew the books were in the prosecutor's hands."

"That's kind of you," Amy said.

She didn't mean it.

Jessop's eyes apologized to me for his daughter, and he said, "I am thankful you got involved and you made the decisions you did. You could easily have walked away. And I know you put yourself at some risk for the sake of the truth."

"Maybe we could petition the government," Amy said, mimicking thoughtfulness, "and get you some kind of medal for bravery. You can spend your time shining it while my dad sits in a prison cell."

For her contribution to the conversation, Sally sobbed at the thought and then busied herself dabbing at her nose with a tissue.

"We're ruined," she said, which was one of the times I knew she was lying to us, because, in fact, she was sitting pretty now with the insurance money, her house, her potential for future romance, and her innate inability to care about others. We ignored her.

Amy said, "What do we do now, wait for the police to lay siege to Dad's house?"

I said to Jessop, "You might want to think about hiring a good lawyer and then turn yourself in. Bail should be reasonable. The legal process is going to take a while. I don't think the law or the community will be crying for blood in the meantime."

"You don't think so?" Amy said. "The church isn't popular at the best of times, and with all those televangelists being exposed, not to mention a few other recent church scandals, the mood is going to be ugly."

"Those were south of the border," I said. "We're more understanding here, or to put it more accurately, most people here don't care what the church is doing."

"The only thing left to do is pray," Jessop said.

I had to agree. He and the church were going for a joyless slide into the abyss, and their only hope was divine intervention.

"He doesn't answer," Amy said.

She was subdued, not even angry, just stating a fact.

"Sometimes He does," Sally said. "I've had prayers answered, even, sometimes, when I didn't know what I wanted."

I didn't want to know the answers she'd received or what she did or didn't know she'd wanted. Her family didn't either.

"He's a mystery," I said. "But you're the expert, Pastor. What do you think?"

"I'm no longer the pastor. You will need to address all your future correspondence to Him personally."

Amy said to me, "Since Father will be too polite to say it, do you think you might excuse us now that you've delivered your enlightening bit of news? We're not inclined to treat you to a cookout around the pool today. Besides, we have personal family matters to discuss."

"I hate to leave, but I know you're busy," I said. "If you need any further help, Larry, just call me, and I'll do what I can."

"Isn't that lovely?" Amy said. "We now know where we can go when we're in trouble."

Amy wasn't going to let me off the hook. I was beginning to believe she didn't like me. Sally showed me to the door, like I'd never been that way before. Then she surprised me.

She said, "Don't worry, she's just upset."

"I thought you were lost in your grief and impending ruin," I said.

"Oh, I hear things," she said, and then closed the door on my dropped jaw.

Sally was a natural at deception. It was second nature to her now. As for me, I was thrilled our get-together was over with. On my way down the mountain, the chick on the radio told me, among her other news items, that Stan Sommers had been released. They didn't have enough evidence to hold him. That meant Stan hadn't been picked as the favorite to take the rap for Brandish. The odds were now running about even Brandish would try to hang Norm around Jessop's neck.

I wasn't eager to face again the all-knowing eyes of the been-there-done-that convert, but it was time to go and ask Mr. Sommers a few questions. I had his number from the church directory, so I phoned from my Hummer to book an appointment. He gave me the *what's the point of wasting our breath?* dodge, but loosened his chaps when I suggested his pastor might be next on the fall-guy list.

He lived in a basement suite on East Hastings, near the exhibition grounds. He let me in and invited me to sit at his kitchen table. He was wearing a chocolate brown bathrobe. His place was decorated in illegal-suite guy décor with a biker clubhouse motif. He got right to the point, like he was nervous sharing his private space with a woman. His eyes were swollen and his sinuses clogged. He was running a fever. He didn't offer me tea.

"Are you all right?" I said.

"Yeah, I'm all right. Jail doesn't agree with me anymore. But there's worse you could catch than the flu."

"It probably doesn't help living underground, either."

Stan ignored my insightful observation.

I said, "I won't keep you, then. So who killed Norman?"

He stared at me for a few seconds and then decided he'd let my bad manners slide.

He said, "I've struggled a lot with my old self since I became a Christian. I don't know what I would have done if it hadn't been for Pastor Jessop. There's a lot of anger I've had to deal with. You probably guessed that, you being the type of person who likes to know things. But that doesn't mean I whacked Norman. Sure, he was a nuisance, but it would take more than that to get me to do something I would regret. I fight all the time to keep my life straight. That's one of the reasons I'm always giving my testimony, so I don't forget where I came from. I don't want my old life to take over again. But I can still feel the anger there. It's something you don't get rid of so easy."

"Thanks for sharing," I said. "So, if it wasn't you or Jessop, who was it?"

"Don't worry, that will all be taken care of. And you can be sure Pastor Jessop isn't going to take the rap, either. You can bet on that."

Stan stuck his chin out and over his brick wall long enough to toss me a brief crooked smile.

"What about your former relationship with Brandish?"

My question slapped Stan's patience. His old self began to stir. It looked like it was getting ready to resurrect itself, and it was. For a few seconds, his face reverted to the image of *biker from hell*, and then saved Stan stuffed the thug back down and slammed the lid. In control again, Stan offered me his tired flu face.

"That's something that just doesn't need going into," he said.

"I won't bother you any further, then. I'd offer to pray for your cold, but healing's not my gift."

"Thanks for the thought," Stan said, and showed me to the door.

I left Stan's basement suite hoping he would never let his old self out to play. If he ever did, I had no doubt his new self wouldn't be the only one to lose.

Back at the office, the afternoon thudded. Bert wasn't answering his cell, and I didn't care. I went home and killed the cat.

* * *

CHAPTER TWELVE

The next morning, I was on a seventeen-straight FreeCell roll when the phone rang. Amy was on the other end, and she hadn't called to wish me well. Her dad had been taken into custody and charged with as many counts of financial wrongdoing as they could think of. At least Norm's murder hadn't made the list. Amy related the news in a jaw-clenched, teeth-grinding style that produced such a lovely, subdued growl that I was proud when she ended her call by addressing me as *Mother*. Next on the line was Sally, who wanted to know the ins and outs of posting bail. I assured her I was available to help her through her ordeal but suggested her father's lawyer was the best person to take care of that detail after her father made his court appearance to enter a plea. She was thankful for that piece of information because she was unable to go out of the house since Norman's funeral and doubted she had the courage to go to the courthouse. My sense this time was that she was telling the truth. Our exchange ended with her blubbering that her poor Norman had left her for real this time, and now her dad was going away too. I half believed her.

I was pushing twenty straight when the phone rang again. It was Braithwaite. He began his slime-speak by mentioning the demise of his late partner, but when he gathered from my silence that his indifference to Stengel's passing was mutual, he didn't pause further to commiserate. He was saddened by Jessop's arrest but saw that it was inevitable given Jessop's reported financial dealings. His oily compassion polluted my ear.

I said, "I haven't heard if they've arrested Brandish yet?"

"Mr. Brandish? Why would they arrest Mr. Brandish?"

"I did take a close look at the books that were delivered to me."

"What books?"

"The financial records Stengel delivered."

"I'm not aware of any financial records he might have given you. I know he handled all the books for the church. My only role was to deposit the weekly tithes and offerings in the bank. I never meddled in his affairs. That was his account. However, I do know he lacked a stomach for business later in life, and then he fell ill. It's a pity."

Dream boat Bert cast off his lines, blew me a kiss, turned, and sailed away. Jessop sat at the dock in a rowboat without oars.

"If none of this is your business, why did you call me?" I said.

"I don't need a reason, do I, Ms. Sunday? But if you must know, I simply wanted to hear your sexy voice quiver as the truth sinks in."

I beeped him off and refocused on finishing my twentieth straight. I did too much thinking. A girl of my quality and attributes needed to enjoy life more. It was tiresome staying ahead of the bad guys. I had enough money. I'd take a part-time job at a cosmetics counter to supplement my stash. Look lovely, sell sparkly blush. I'd forget about men, or maybe not. Life would be easy. I exited FreeCell in mid-twenty-one. I was embarrassed about Bert, and I was a failure at my profession. I'd been set up to further the goals of Mr. Brandish, whatever they were. So had the sick man Stengel. At least he died believing he'd done the deed, but his futile redemption attempt was a disaster for Jessop. And Bert, my dear Bert, executed the old switcheroo. The original records of Brandish's crimes were now shreds, evidence had been substituted crucifying Jessop, and to scrub the money trail clean, Stengel's farewell ride on the planet had been cut short. Brandish killed his own church that laid the golden egg, and his gray sedan killed Stengel and Norm, but there was no motive. Norm was no threat to Brandish's power. He had Jessop fronting his corruption, and he had pastors galore waiting in the prayer room to fill Jessop's robes. I was no threat. There were crimes committed, without a motive, and crimes exposed for no reason. There was a chance God did it, but my lack of theological training precluded me from explaining that to the judge. I wished Dad were here and then remembered I didn't. My choices were to face Brandish or to sharpen my people skills for clerk duty. I chose Brandish. I phoned, and his secretary said he was on another line, but he had an opening at one o'clock. I said I'd be pleased to fill it.

When I arrived, his secretary forgot to be sweet. I thumbed through *People* and tossed it in favor of the objects in *Better Homes and Gardens*. Brandish toddled out a few minutes after one o'clock, wearing his mouse-for-lunch grin. He beckoned me to join him in his flashy lair. I walked in ahead of him, thankful he was slow on his feet. I was doing my best impression of a tough broad, but my soft skin and gentle heart gave me away. It was something I had to live with. He invited me to sit in his lounge area. I chose one of his stuffed chairs, and he occupied the love seat.

He said, "You really don't understand what this is all about, do you?"

"I think I do. You're a megalomaniac with a narcissistic bent."

"We majored in psychology, did we, Jane?"

"Yes, Alec, my father taught me the course in grade three, at the track between races."

"I must say you have been wearing my patience a little thin."

He was lying to make me feel good. Plus I had a good idea his layer of patience hadn't been too thick to begin with.

"You should have told me sooner," I said. "I hate to be a bother."

"I see. Well, let's start again, shall we? Let me begin by giving you an essential lesson in the facts of life. Contrary to the prevailing view of the parishioners on Sunday morning, the church is virtually insignificant in the broad scope of commerce and trade that this province of BC and this great country are all about. And men like Pastor Jessop are expendable when so much is at stake."

"And Norman Parks and Benjamin Stengel, I suppose they're hardly worth a mention?"

"Now you are beginning to understand, and I am sorry about your boyfriend. Bert has had a problem for years. He tried, but lifelong habits are difficult to break. It's only a pot addiction, but it renders him useless most days to perform his duties. Because he is taken care of by my good graces, he is agreeable to undertake certain tasks for me from time to time, although I really don't think of you as a task. You're much too special for that."

I had to agree I was special, but Brandish was fabricating his Bert story. Bert might have played lover and errand boy, but he wasn't a pothead. I'd seen a lot of them, and Bert wasn't one.

I said, "What's this all about, then? You can level with me."

"It wouldn't be fair for me to explain all the details to you. That would spoil the fun you overcurious people seem to thrive on by trying to figure these things out. So I'll give you a hint in the form of a question. Why do you think nobody has stopped me from destroying the church and Pastor Jessop?"

"You're the Antichrist?"

"I see. Well, it has been enjoyable to have you along on this part of our journey. It was only chance that Norman hired you, but you have served us very well, I must admit. It was enjoyable for me and convenient for us to have such a gifted woman further our cause. And, if and when you come to realize where your best interests lie, I am sure I can easily arrange a permanent role for you in our organization, one that suits your gifts and talents. There is also the potential for you and me to have a meaningful time together in the process."

"Don't get your hopes up. I'm packing bug spray in my purse."

"I was afraid you were going to take that attitude. I'm saddened by your lack of insight into present truths. The future might go very well for you, but not in your current state. I know that time and events will serve to open your eyes."

"You'll still look the same, Alec. And Bert's not a pot-head."

"I hope you enjoyed following my exploits in the records you received from Stengel. It is too bad they didn't make it to the prosecutor's office. The ones they did receive had Pastor Jessop's signature throughout. It's like getting away with murder, isn't it?"

"Thank you for confirming that for me. It will look good in my report."

"I'm afraid it will be a sad realization for you when you discover there will be no one interested in reading your account of recent proceedings. And thank you for not bringing a recording device with you, although our security would have detected it anyway."

"Your hospitality, as always, has been heartwarming. Forgive me, but I must go now and arrange for your descent to hell."

"I am truly sorry that you see me in such a negative light."

Brandish grunted and pushed himself up from his seat. I stood and retreated from his heavy breathing.

"But let's stay friends, shall we?" he said.

He swung his stubby arm toward me. His hand on the end of it hoped for contact with one of my soft parts.

I said, "Thank you, I'd shake it, but I don't know where it's been."

I backed away until I reached the door. He tried to overtake me, but his little feet couldn't pitter-patter fast enough. I was gone. His secretary was talking on her headset when I glided by and was neither surprised by my desire to leave nor much interested in my passing.

My ride back to the office was punctuated with periods of doubt and light rain. My doubts shot the breeze with my little-girl self, and the rain fell because that's what rain did. Brandish remained free to hawk his wares, but Jessop had been forced to pencil in a long sabbatical. And even though I knew Brandish's version of Bert-the-pothead was a sadistic lie, my little-girl self was struggling to clasp the hope Bert's shining armor wasn't a rental. To inflate himself further, Brandish had confessed to me. That was his mistake, and I'd also taken out some added insurance to cover my bets. There was a season for everything, even for Brandish's time to rupture. I was required to love my enemies, but I allowed the image to linger of his guts splattering his office walls. I was beginning to think I didn't have a Christian attitude.

I squeezed my machine into a parking spot on Hornby Street and took the stairs to the second floor, where I found Bert's place of employment. We had business to discuss.

I asked the receptionist to give him a buzz and let him know his sister was here with family news of a disturbing kind. Bert's head smirked out from the door to his office, and I was granted admission. He closed the door and grabbed hold of me, which was no way to treat his sister, but I didn't mind. He had my number, and I lacked the integrity to unlist it now. He continued to get personal in a hurry. After an amiable interval, I used my elbows to signal time out.

"I've never had such an exciting visitor in here," he said.

I could see he meant it, and then we both sat down.

"I'll have to drop around more often to make sure things get where they're supposed to go."

"You don't know how the system works," he said.

"Your system seems to be working fine."

"I delivered the package you gave me."

Those were the words I wanted to hear. He knew that too. My emotions decided to believe him. I put my cautious mind on hold and made it listen to my heart's beautiful music.

I said, "Why does Brandish insist you've got a drug problem?"

"I'm sure you might have noticed he's not a kind man. I did do some cocaine in my younger days, but those days are gone."

Bert was telling me the truth, or he was Pinocchio-the-snorter minus the long bloody nose. But since Brandish had taken the trouble to slander him, the odds were ten to one Bert was shooting straight. My heart decided to trust its future beating to my man. Otherwise life wasn't worth the wait.

"How did it happen, then?"

"He's got people in this ministry. His influence extends into government and the media. Who knows? They're all serving the bottom line. But there are some good people serving it, because that's all they know how to do."

"What are you serving?"

"I don't care about it anymore. How about you? Are you in need of a servant?"

"None of this makes any sense. He's skewered the shepherd and the sheep and is about to roast them over an open fire when they are still useful to him. As for our involvement, he didn't need our help. There has to be a reason."

"He's an evil man. Evil doesn't need a reason."

"Is there anyone you can trust in the AG's Ministry who has some influence and isn't on Brandish's payroll?"

"Why, what have you got? You mean you've been holding out on us?"

"I'm not giving up on this," I said. "Brandish isn't immune to his own folly."

"I'm glad you haven't given up on me."

"Go easy. We've got a long way to go before we're free to be fruitful and multiply."

"We're too old for that," he said.

"I wouldn't mind going through the motions as long as you make an honest woman out of me."

"As we both know by now, love is sacrificial, but I'm more than willing to make that sacrifice."

"This would be a bad time to get killed," I said.

"If we have to go, let's make sure we go together."

"You're so romantic."

Bert closed the distance between us and met me coming his way. I loved the view of our future shining in Bert's eyes.

The temptation to propose to Bert that we relocate to Fiji came and went.

I said, "If we walked away from Jessop, we'd never be able to shake off our regrets."

"He's a good man, but he's susceptible like the rest of us."

"We all need to wake up before the bad guys are us," I said.

"Are you available to discuss our future over dinner tonight?"

"Okay, I get the hint. I'm leaving. There are probably a few people wondering what you're doing in here with your sister at the taxpayers' expense. And I am happy to hear that I'm not just one of your assignments."

"I'll call you later," he said, and we sealed the deal.

On my way out, the receptionist nodded, acknowledging my glow and glad my emergency had passed. Outside, the clouds had parted, and the blue sky tickled me inside; an image appeared from the past of the innocent me, a delighted girl spinning in a daisy field. I would have giggled at the passersby, but that wasn't what a mature private investigator did when she was out in public.

On the road back to my office, dear Amy rang my cell to let me know her dad had made bail, no thanks to me. She further instructed me to stay away from her and the family. I asked if I was now excommunicated since I wouldn't, under her prohibition, be allowed to attend church. She pointed out that, thanks to me, the church wasn't long for this world anyway. I said I would consider her orders and follow them when I thought it was advisable. In response to my request, she was agreeable, under protest, to meet me for coffee at the White Spot so that we might have the opportunity to discuss in person her view of our relationship. I sensed she missed her mother and needed someone to talk to. Amy was starting to grow on me.

I expected her to be her usual self, her sharp edges cutting whatever came close, but when I arrived, she was already in a booth, stirring her strawberry shake with her straw and looking like she wanted to bawl. I invited myself to sit down and then waited.

"None of it's fair," she said. "We didn't have a chance, when I look back on it. Mom and Dad had a miserable time together. He was always busy with the church. She wasn't suited to be a pastor's wife. She lacked ambition as far as the church went and took a backseat in spiritual matters. I don't think she really understood it all and why my dad was so consumed by it. They were a mismatch really, but she made the most of it. And then she's gone, and now Dad's going to jail, Sally's disintegrating whether she knows it or not, and I don't know where I'm going or what I'm supposed to do."

Her last admission melted her cool, and the tears began to drip. A couple of hiccupped sobs followed. Our server, who'd been around the block a thousand times and seen it all before, pouted one corner of her mouth at Amy in polite sympathy and asked me what I would like. I would have liked to give Amy a hug, but I was short of experience in the mothering thing.

"Bring me what she's having," I said.

"A strawberry shake and a Legendary," she said, and jotted it on her pad and then left for a sunnier table.

I'd already expected Amy was going to grow on me, and now the worst had happened. I'd gone soft. The words jostled for position and then stumbled out.

I said, "I could use a secretary. It would give you something to do while you're waiting for Hollywood to come knocking."

"Are you serious?" she said, and blew her cute red nose into her napkin.

I wasn't sure whether she meant the idea was absurd and beneath her dignity or whether she thought I was mocking her.

"Have you had any secretarial experience?" I said. "I know you have a university degree and been to film school, but can you do anything?"

"How hard could it be?" she said.

She squirmed and then began to poke her shake bubbles with her straw. Then I realized Amy had left her superior attitude in her other jeans.

To help break her fall into humility, I said, "Oh, I see. You're thinking you might spy on me?"

"There must be something we can do about Dad."

"I do have a few ideas. Mr. Brandish is not invincible."

"I knew it. You have been keeping secrets."

Amy ditched her pain and tears and was ready to run with the hounds.

"So you do want the job? I presume that important position you applied for in the movie racket hasn't come through yet?"

"I haven't heard anything, but that doesn't mean I won't. In the meantime, I guess anything is better than nothing."

"You're probably going to be my downfall, but I'll take the chance. I'll think of it as my contribution toward helping out the next generation. And I suppose, while you're at it, you'll want to learn a few things about the detective business?"

"Don't worry," she said. "It's only temporary, till something better comes along."

"You're hired. You'll make enough to pay the rent and keep your escapist self floating in Bloody Caesars."

"Poverty will be a small price to pay for the privilege of working at the feet of an ace detective."

Something told me my FreeCell game was going to suffer.

"You can start tomorrow," I said.

"You work on Saturday?"

"Get used to it."

* * *

CHAPTER THIRTEEN

Back at my office, I clicked and scanned the local news on the Internet. Jessop and the church were running the gauntlet and taking a beating. The beaters were screaming they'd had enough of church tax privileges, and why didn't the government do something about tax exemptions on church property and donations? One pundit, an atheist by trade, wanted to know why churches weren't made to suffer like the rest of us and pay their fair share. And why did Christians get a break on tax-deductible donations? Recovery of that lost income alone had the potential to make a huge dent in the national debt. But he maintained, of course, that there were legitimate nonprofit organizations that belonged in a separate category and should retain their tax breaks. It was the delusional Christians who were abusing the system, and they were an exclusive and discriminatory group besides, especially those who were opposed to gay rights and a woman's right to choose. As an afterthought, he tossed in that everyone, including Pastor Jessop, of course, was innocent until proven guilty. His main points made, his proud conclusion was that millions of Canadians, and the country as a whole, would benefit from the revoking of such an archaic provision in the Income Tax Act.

The pot was boiling and waiting for the Christians to be stripped and plopped in.

I knew it was time to step out and risk the business again. I had a couple of hidden stones left to sling at Brandish. I knew he must have heard of a photocopier sometime in his life, but then maybe his arrogant view from the penthouse had overlooked or ignored the actions of the little people for so long that he'd become careless. And as a courtesy, I'd send him an e-mail to recommend a new security system for his office. Unless Brandish knew something I didn't and was playing me for sport, I had the goods, and I had to deliver them to the place where they would get the most attention. Since I'd sunk my life into Bert, he and I needed to talk about the wheels within wheels inside the AG's office. But I needed to change the lock on my emotions. Bert had found the combination and slipped his way in, which hadn't been that tough since I'd volunteered the numbers, and next Amy had pried me open and touched my soft heart. I'd included her in my life now, and that would leave me vulnerable to her pointed questions about the case. She would want to know a few particulars, especially the ones that concerned her dad's uncertain future. As for Jessop, he was someone I had to talk to again soon. But first Bert and I were on course tonight to mix business with pleasure.

It was my first visit to his place of rest in the Shangri-La on Georgia, a high-end condo for the well-heeled. It was the tallest tower in Vancouver. The luxury vibe started in the lobby. It was three stories high with six crystal chandeliers. The floors and walls were limestone with some rosewood paneling added for comfort. The plush leather club chairs for the weary rich sat empty. I phoned up, and he met me at the elevator on the fifty-first floor. After our chummy greeting, he walked me through his two-story sky loft. The thirty-foot ceilings were a nice touch. The lights on the North Shore Mountains and the city lights below shone in the night, like they were sparkling to be noticed and were ready to serve. He had his own home theater off the kitchen, and his master bedroom was big enough to gobble my whole town house. Bert needed to repent, but I wasn't going to be the one to tell him. After the tour and a snuggle on the couch overlooking the world, he invited me to his table.

"You must have saved your pennies," I said.

He'd catered dinner in my favorite basic Chinese.

"It's an investment. Do you think you can learn to love it?"

"I suppose vertigo is something you can get used to."

I expected a houseboy to spring from the kitchen to pass the dishes around, but we managed to do it instead.

I was making good use of the chopsticks when Bert said, "What is it that you're not telling me?"

"The deep-fried wontons are exceptional."

"It has to be an ironclad case," he said. "No one is going to stick their neck out for nothing."

"Who do you trust at work, someone who might be able to get the job done if they had the right information?"

"There's Jillian. She coordinates the ministry, and she's been there for years. I don't think she's corruptible. I don't know how much power she has if it came to a showdown. Why, what have you got?"

"I've got photocopies of the original church financial documents and audio of Brandish implicating himself."

I could see that Bert was proud of me.

"You don't fool around, do you? If you would like, I can arrange a meeting for you with Jillian. I'm not taking the responsibility this time for lost and replaced articles. And you might need to get yourself a lawyer."

"You are a lawyer."

"I have a conflict of interest, wouldn't you say?"

"Do you have any conflict over me?"

"No, I'm solid on you."

We enjoyed our dinner, and then Bert took me into his theater. We watched *Casablanca*. I fell asleep after. Bert woke me with a kiss. He didn't mention if I snored.

"Are you sure I'm not just another one of your girls?" I said in my bedroom voice.

"You're a keeper. And I'll say it again. When you're ready, I'd like to make our arrangement permanent. I couldn't be more excited about the prospect."

"That sounds like a proposal, but it might be lawyer talk for something else."

"It's a proposal," he said, and kissed my ear. He added, "We Christians of a certain age shouldn't bother wasting too much time on the preliminaries, especially since cohabitation is no longer an option for us."

"I hear you. But I think I'm going to pretend to be undecided for six months or so. I don't want you to think I'm jumping at the offer."

"Fair enough, as long as you're only pretending."

It was time for me to make my getaway. We said our good-byes. They took a while.

The next morning I phoned Jessop. He stuttered between thoughts like he was in the middle of a sermon and he'd lost his place. He agreed to see me. Amy had yet to arrive at the office for her first day on the job. I left her a note commending her on her punctuality and advising her to clean the office from the bottom up. On the way over to Jessop's, I picked up the gray sedan. It looked like I was once again a person of interest to Brandish. He followed me to Jessop's house in Point Grey but decided not to enter the driveway for a formal visit. I was just as happy. Jessop's housekeeper answered the door tut-tutting and led me into his study, shaking her head. The curtains were wide open. He was smiling in the dusty light. The room itself needed a gentle beating, like you'd clean an old, gritty rug.

"I'm delighted to see you," he said. "How are you and my friend Bert getting along?"

Jessop was too joyful for his own good.

"We are proceeding to our desired destination."

"And would that destination be marriage?"

"That is a possibility."

"If and when you decide, and if my trip to prison is delayed, I would love to do the wedding."

He beamed in the light.

I noted Pastor Larry was over the edge. Our time together was destined to be filed under *non compos mentis.*

"I came to let you know there is some hope," I said.

"There is only one hope, my dear, and our Savior is it."

"Generally, I agree with you, but I'm talking more specifically about your legal situation."

"I'm going to jail for adultery."

Jessop nodded in agreement with himself.

"They don't put you in jail for adultery."

"God does. Just ask Him. Spiritual adultery. I'll probably get ten to twenty years for putting other gods before Him."

Then he sang, "God of self, god of mammon, god of success, all gods before him."

"Nice tune, but I came to talk about Brandish. I have evidence that will put him away for a long time."

"Oh, good, we can be cell mates. I get the top bunk."

"Have you talked to your daughters since you've been out?"

"Only on the phone. They can't come over, not yet. I told them that I'm fine."

"There's a good chance you're going to get off light, probation maybe."

"Oh, good, I'll take probation light. It's nonfattening. But then what? Cynthia's gone, you know. There's nothing to do."

"Do you have anyone you can call, a pastor maybe, for you to talk to?"

"I'm the pastor. I take care of people. Didn't you know? And, so sad, there is no one to take care of me."

Jessop reflected on his conundrum and didn't notice me excuse myself to call Amy. She said she'd arrived late at the office because her dog had eaten her homework. She informed me no one had called and then asked if anybody ever did call and was cleaning the office all she was hired to do? I explained her dad's condition to her. She understood and said she'd be right over if her boss permitted her to leave before she finished mopping the floor. I said her immediate presence was requested and hung up. I asked the housekeeper how long Jessop had been in this condition. She said he'd been up all night, sitting at his desk and moaning. In the morning he'd opened the curtains wide for the first time in months and began to sing nonsense songs and giggle. She thought at first that his change in mood was a positive sign, but could see now that it wasn't much of an improvement. I rejoined Jessop in his study and waited for Amy.

"You're back," he said. "I missed you. You are a lovely person. Are you a believer really?"

"I must be. Why else would I put up with the church?"

"We all see the mess we've made. Yes, we see the sickness. I suppose you couldn't miss it."

"I have a question for you."

"Oh, good, twenty questions, fire away. Cynthia and the kids and I used to have fun like this. She's gone now. Brandish made sure of that."

"You'll have to testify against Brandish. Are you willing?"

"Aren't we getting ahead of ourselves, Jane? You haven't got him caught yet, have you?"

"Do you have a doctor you can call?" I said.

"Yes, let's call my doctor, good idea. It's a revelation you have had. He can put me on drugs, and then I will be all better."

My sense was that Jessop had been medicated before, which explained daughter Sally's urge to follow in her father's footsteps.

"Amy is coming over," I said.

"Oh, excellent, Amy is the smart one. She will take care of things. She's mad at Him now because of me, but she's a believer. Did you know there are Christians in the church, real believers? There aren't that many, but they're there. They will make it through okay. Their faith doesn't depend on me. It's their own faith. Extraordinary, isn't it? See, I can't take the blame for everything."

Jessop faced the light and grinned. His mind had played enough for now. He was at peace. I left him there and went to wait for Amy in the front hall, where I would have a better view of the gray sedan. Amy drove in about ten minutes later, her old white Rabbit blowing blue diesel exhaust behind her. The housekeeper, jealous for her job, churned past me and opened the door.

"Hi, Rosa," Amy said.

At me she frowned.

"He's in his study," Rosa said, ignoring me. It was clear I wasn't included in their home club.

"Did he go off his medication?" Amy said.

"He must have," Rosa said.

"I'll take care of it," Amy said.

In silence she led me back to his study to show me she was the one in charge in her father's house. I cooperated. When we entered, I saw that Jessop had maintained his sunny outlook. Enraptured in the light, he broke his muse in two stages. He looked at Amy and then back out the window. A few seconds later, he looked back and recognized her.

"Amy," he said, "we were just talking about you, and here you are."

She went over to his chair and gave his head a hug.

"I'm going to get your pills," she said.

He seemed fine with that, and she left on her errand of mercy.

"She is a lovely girl," Jessop said to me. "I am going to miss her."

His sentiment was self-indulgent.

"She's working for me now," I said. "I needed a secretary, and she agreed to take the job."

"I think I will fill in the pool," he said.

I felt embarrassed for attempting small talk with a no-track mind. Amy returned with pills and glass of water in hand.

"When was the last time you took your medication, Dad?" she said.

"And then I will plant grass," he said.

Jessop took his medicine from firm Amy, turned on his desk lamp, and then stood and closed the curtains.

"Oh, never mind, there was no point to it anyway," he said and returned to his chair.

For their information, I said, "I have copies of the original church financial records Stengel gave me, not the forged ones that were switched. They're enough to convict Brandish, and I also have his admission of guilt recorded."

Amy said, "You mean they got the wrong records and my dad's current condition could have been prevented? Why didn't the right ones go to the authorities in the first place, and when are you going to correct that minor little error?"

Jessop said, "The Lord works in mysterious ways. There's nobody to blame…nobody to blame. But I'm glad Jane and Bert are heading for bliss. He's a good man. Well done, Jane, well done."

Amy wasn't as happy for me.

"Why don't you go upstairs and lie down, Dad? You need to get some sleep."

"I won't argue. I will go peacefully, a lamb to the slaughter, but not an innocent one. And my sacrifice will go for nothing. So be it. Don't worry. I'm gone."

Jessop left the room holding himself guilty. Amy jerked open the curtains.

She said, "I don't suppose it's my place to reprimand my boss."

"Go ahead if it makes you feel better. If you think I'm the one who pushed your family's self-destruct button, say it."

"As if. Could you be any more sensitive? And nice martyr's complex too. Who gave you the right to think you could take responsibility for my family? But I am delighted to hear you and your boyfriend kissed and made up. Why don't you and Bert take off for Mexico and forget any of this happened?"

"I have to stay here and finish the job. I'm caught up with the sense of my own importance. And I'd like to see justice done, too."

"A private detective with a conscience, what a wonderful concept."

"I'm not going to fire you, so you might as well stop trying, at least not until you've cleaned the office."

Amy shifted gears. "You can keep him out of jail, can't you?"

"How's this? I'll keep him from doing time, or die trying. How does that suit you?"

"How much are you paying me anyway?"

"More than you're worth. Now let's go. You can leave your rust bucket here and come with me. You can pick it up later. There's a car outside on the street that's waiting for us."

"You're the boss."

Amy and I exited the driveway in my Hummer at about twenty-five miles per hour. My left front bumper crumpled the gray sedan's right front just enough to prevent its wheel from turning. The glancing collision added inspiration to my sharp right turn, and I accelerated down the street toward our next destination. I saw no reason to stop and render assistance.

"Where did you learn how to drive?" Amy said.

"Toronto," I said, and eased off the gas.

I took Amy back to the office under protest. She saw no reason why she shouldn't tag along with me. I reminded her of her cleaning duties. She mumbled that endearing word, *Mother*, again. I was touched.

* * *

CHAPTER FOURTEEN

I could hardly wait for church Sunday. Bert and I made the trip together. The sad sheep had packed the pews to hear it wasn't so. Amy and Sally were absent. Brandish opened the meeting with the tragic story of Pastor Jessop's sins. Beneath the grieving pose of his slug flesh, I saw that the soul of Brandish was thrilled to give them the bad news. He ended his tale by telling us that he and the board would see us through this trying time. Therefore we were not to despair, because there were even better days ahead. In conclusion, he said that if anyone had any questions, they were best submitted in written form and delivered to the office, or given to a board member, or placed in the offering basket. The deed done, and immediate chaos averted, Brandish departed for his pew. Next the music director invited us to stand for the first chorus. Half of us did. The other half sat on their wallets and clutched their purses. The director, singers, and musicians tried to lift us, but the congregation remained earthbound. Her duty clear, she led the moaning crowd through the full program. The offering followed. None of the ushers was injured when they passed the plates, although growls could be heard.

Bert said, "The pew is uncomfortable this morning."

"But he won't get away with it for long, will he?" I said.

"We live in hope."

Pastor Gerard took the pulpit in relief, but nothing he pitched this morning was even considered. The congregation was ready to walk. Having finished what he came to deliver, he sensed the game was over and closed the meeting with a prayer. Nobody lamented the axing of the closing hymn. Brandish and Braithwaite made their getaway in tandem, the fat man slowing the lean. The angry and grumbling sheep collected in groups, made decisions, and then voted with their feet, exiting the sanctuary in droves and not stopping in the foyer for refreshments. In the parking lot, horns honked. Betrayal was hard to forgive. I felt lighter after we left the crucifixion site.

"Where do we go from here?" Bert said.

"You're driving. You'd better know where we're going."

"You're the one who's been giving the directions so far," he said.

"That's great, an argument. We're getting right into the spirit of the morning."

"When anger is in the air, it's easy to catch. We need to clean ourselves off."

"How about we clean each other off instead?"

"Your place or mine?"

"Have you got any more of those old classic movies?"

* * *

Tuesday morning book club labored like the turtle in our current pick, *The Grapes of Wrath*. Lily decided that Steinbeck was promoting the notion that the salvation of mankind depended on people coming together to unite for the common good.

"There is always hope for us," she said. "If we keep on pushing, if we keep on trying, despite the odds, we will succeed."

Lily squinted, like she was trying to see her way west through prairie topsoil blowing in the hot wind.

"If all of us would only come together," she said.

"What are you suggesting," Winnie said, "salvation by works? What about the gospel?"

Elsa said, "Let's try to keep the gospel out of this discussion for once. We're studying literature, remember?"

"But what about this Jim Casy character?" Winnie said. "His initials are J.C. What was Steinbeck trying to say there?"

"There you go again," Elsa said. "You're indefatigable when it comes to the gospel." Elsa was proud of her long word. We tried not to be embarrassed for her.

"How are we going to avoid it?" Winnie said. "Religion is in everything. And the title, *The Grapes of Wrath*, everyone knows that's from the Book of Revelations."

"It's the Book of Revelation," Anne said. "There's no *s* on the end. Everyone always makes that mistake."

"Let's start again," Elsa said. "We have begun this morning on the wrong foot once more. Surely there are themes we can discuss that do not lead us back down that old, familiar trail to religion. Our faith is not in question here. We don't have to spend our time examining it or defending it. There are other areas we can focus on."

"I agree," Lily said. "Love is what we need, and I think Steinbeck points to the family and our relationships with others as the means to salvation."

I felt inspired to ask, "What about evil?"

"What did your SparkNotes say about it?" Elsa said.

She'd decided to be snotty this morning.

I was just as happy and said, "That the novel points to economic injustice as the primary source of evil and suffering in the world, the *haves* lording it over the *have-nots*."

"Bravo," Elsa said. "Excellent memorizing."

"The devil is the source of all evil," Winnie said.

"That's not altogether true," Anne said. "We can make our own choices, and we are the ones who are responsible when we make evil choices."

"Yes," Lily said. "That's the whole point. We are responsible for the evil and suffering in the world. Love is the only answer. We need to learn to love one another. Look at the Joads."

"Look at the Joads' what?" Winnie said.

"They are a family," Lily said, "and then they are an extended family, and then they are part of a social group fighting for justice against the tyranny of the landowners. They had to unite to survive."

"Not like us," Anne said.

"Not like whom?" Elsa said.

"You know," Anne said.

"Go ahead and say it," Elsa said.

"Okay, the church, we're not united," Anne said.

"I know we are going through a time of troubles right now with the leadership and the church finances," Elsa said, "but if we stand together, we will be fine."

"We aren't standing together," Anne said. "People are deserting right, left, and center. Most of them are planning to go to other churches."

"We aren't really a family," Winnie said, "or an extended family. If we were, we would stick together."

"It's Brandish," I said.

"What do you mean?" Elsa said. "What does Mr. Brandish have to do with it?"

"He's the evil landowner," I said.

"That is the kind of offensive, unsubstantiated remark that leads to gossip," Elsa said, "and we all know that gossip causes serious damage to church unity."

"But it's true," I said.

"There is no point in continuing this morning," Elsa said. "There are forces at work determined to undermine any legitimate attempt to study the novel in depth. I suggest we all reconsider the work and our attitudes and come prepared next week to examine the text in a more disciplined way. For those who haven't read the book, or for those who have not quite finished it, this cooling-off period will give you ample time to finish that task. Any questions?"

"I thought the movie was excellent," Anne said, "even in black-and-white."

"That is not a question," Elsa said.

"Henry Fonda was excellent in it, too," Winnie said.

"It looks like our troubles in the church have also infected our little group," Lily said.

"Don't you see?" Anne said. "We have always been on the verge of falling apart. Our membership in this thing we call the church has been holding us together. But now what do we do?"

"Study literature," Elsa said. "That is why we organized this group."

"I thought we were coming together because we are Christians," Anne said.

"There she goes again," Elsa said. "Anne, you are incorrigible."

Elsa then laughed like our rift was trivial.

An impulse to be the peacemaker popped out. I said, "I think I'll try to read the whole book by next week."

"That is wonderful," Lily said. "I knew you had it in you."

Lily smiled and nodded at the rest of the group, like she'd told them so.

"What a nice gesture," Elsa said.

She was flicking snot again, but the others didn't see it, or that she was aiming it at me.

"We can all learn to live together in peace and harmony," Lily said.

In the spirit of the moment, Anne and Winnie deferred comment about salvation by works. We disbanded without further controversy.

I'd arranged an afternoon meeting with Bert and his colleague Jillian Campbell at his Shangri-la. They were waiting when I arrived. She was a petite redhead on her way to retirement. She looked sweet, but I sensed her sparkling light blue eyes hid a killer inside. She was the right woman for the job. Gentleman Bert introduced us and slipped me a wink instead of a kiss. It was his way of promising that I'd be able to collect something more substantial later.

Jillian took charge. She said, "Bert has given me the details. You have copies of the original church financial records and audio of Mr. Brandish implicating himself in fraud and murder. Is that right?"

"They're not concealed in my panty hose, but, yes, I do have them in my possession."

"And you are ready to turn this evidence over to the Crown Prosecutor's Office?"

"Yes, I'm ready. Are you? Our last effort didn't go so well."

"Mr. Brandish has his stooges everywhere, but not everyone is on his payroll."

"Thank goodness, my faith in the system has been restored. How do I know this isn't just another dance with deception?"

Bert twitched his lip at me. He either resented the intimation or was registering his criticism of my lame turn of phrase.

"Bert has told me you two are more than friends. You have to trust someone, or you will be dancing alone."

I liked Jillian's answer, and I liked Jillian. She was weary enough with life to be trusted.

"Where and when would you like the evidence delivered?"

"You might have saved some time by having it with you today," she said.

Jillian had paid her dues, so I didn't mind her chastising me.

I said to Bert, "The gray sedan resumed his interest in me today. It's likely Brandish has this place bugged."

"Why did you agree to meet here then?" Bert said.

I could see that Jillian wanted to know too.

"I'd like to see him make a few more mistakes."

"It was nice of you to include me," Jillian said.

"If you give me your number," I said, "I'll call you on your cell to arrange the delivery."

"It has been a pleasure meeting you, Ms. Sunday. I look forward to hearing from you soon."

She handed me her card.

"As do I," Bert said and then, aware of his corny tone, decided to embellish it further, saying to Jillian, "Shall we?"

Jillian raised an eyebrow.

We departed Shangri-La for our respective offices. The gray sedan was now black. He'd gotten moody. I called Jillian on her cell and told her I'd hand over the package at The

Last Drop coffee shop down the street from her office on Hornby at two o'clock. She agreed.

Back at the office, I found Amy making herself comfortable in my chair, reading *Cosmopolitan*. She'd done a good job on the floor Saturday—she missed coming in Monday, something about losing her car keys—and today the rest of the place looked clean too.

"Nice job," I said. "Now get out of my chair."

She stood and returned the magazine to the stack. I reclaimed my territory.

"There are some great tips in there for luring the opposite sex. I assume that's how you caught Bert. But is that the kind of material a middle-aged Christian gal should be reading?"

"It's that or enter a convent. Have there been any calls?"

"No, I don't think anyone knows you're here," she said, and plunked her cheeky jeans on my desk. "Perhaps you should advertise."

"I've got enough work to last me for a while."

"Are you going to let me know what's going on, or do I just guess? I know it's only the second day, but you haven't done a very good job of mentoring so far, unless you are counting your lesson in bumper cars, and that wasn't a very good example to set, either."

"I'm turning over the evidence to the prosecutor's office today. And then we'll see what happens next. If Brandish is charged, it will be a start. If he isn't, I'm going to take a long holiday on the French Riviera."

"Alone?"

"Unless you're coming."

"I'll be here, thanks, still trying to help my dad. But if your plan fails, I take it there will be no Bert with you, either? So sad."

"Let's hope it doesn't go that way. It's lunchtime. Are you coming?"

"Are you sure the big boss should be lunching with the little employee?"

"I'll make an exception this time."

The black sedan followed us to our favorite White Spot. I planned to go straight from there to meet Jillian. We took our time eating. Amy had the usual on her mind. She massaged recent history for about ten minutes to relax her tension and then made a positive prognosis.

"Dad is going to get off. I know it," she said.

My cell rang. It was Brandish offering me, in the form of a question, an insight into my possible future.

"You don't suppose you're going to escape unscathed for causing me this trouble, do you?"

"I was hoping you'd let bygones be bygones and send me on a free trip to Disneyland before you begin your slide into oblivion."

"I see. Well, I'm not suggesting anything will happen to *you* at the moment. I enjoy knowing that you are alive and well and that you will soon come to realize the error of your ways. My hope grows daily that we will see eye to eye in the very near future. If not, well, there are no guarantees in life. In the meantime, as I said, there will be ramifications for your behavior."

I beeped him off.

"Was that Brandish?" Amy said.

"Yes, he says he likes me."

"He's going to try and stop you."

"I'm not worried. The word on the street is that heaven is better than this and that all I'll need is a change of outfit."

"But what about me?"

"You will still be you."

Amy let me pay the bill. I was happy to do it. I took her with me for the ride to meet Jillian. Having her sitting there beside me felt natural, like she'd been there her whole life. I hated vulnerability.

"Get your feet off the dash," I said, "and buckle your seat belt."

She decided not to hear me.

The black sedan was getting pushy. He threatened my rear a couple of times, like he was holding a grudge. Amy saw him in the side mirror, dropped her feet to the floor, and buckled her belt.

"I told you Brandish would try to stop you," she said.

"This guy's only flirting. I'll let him know his advances are hopeless."

I shot him some exhaust. He wasn't discouraged; he caught up and then pulled alongside. I expected a nudge, but at least he wasn't that rude. Amy eyeballed him and said he was grinning. I'd misjudged him. He did have a sense of humor. While it was an endearing trait, it was unprofessional. I'd have to report him to his boss. I asked Amy to take his picture with the camera in the glove box while he was in a photogenic mood. She did. Our vehicles arrived together on Hornby Street, joined at the doors. I saw a spot, braked, pulled in behind him, and parked. He could find his own space.

"Stay here," I said.

I removed the package from a compartment beneath the dash. Amy said she wasn't going to let me out of her sight. I felt wanted. We walked to The Last Drop, where Jillian was already waiting, coffee in hand. We joined her at her table.

I wasn't thirsty. Amy kicked me under the table when she saw the grinning man enter. I passed the package to Jillian, who shoved it into her briefcase. The big man, minus his black sedan, came straight at us. I emptied Jillian's hot coffee into his face and swung my chair's wrought iron frame through the space his head occupied. He fell like a rotten old-growth tree in the forest. We heard his head hit the floor. I looked down and saw that his toothy grin was missing. Jillian decided it was time for her to leave. I told her I owed her a coffee, but she wasn't worried about it. We left the rubble for the owner to sweep up. Outside, I took a deep breath and readjusted my bra.

Amy was calm but impressed. Back in my Hummer, she said, "You're meaner than I thought you were."

"I've been a victim before," I said, and pulled into traffic. "And I don't like it."

"You know, I think we do have a chance," she said, like she'd had a revelation.

"If we don't," I said, "there's not much hope for any of us."

"Who's us?" she said, and put her feet back up on the dash.

* * *

Bert broke it to me on the phone the next morning. Brandish had been taken in for questioning. Jillian and my man Bert had gotten the job done. I was happier about Bert being true blue than hearing about Brandish's barrel roll on his glide path to hell. Amy was late again, so I was dancing alone with the news. The black sedan hadn't shown for work this morning, either. His orthodontist must have had an opening. Amy arrived an hour late, but I didn't even pretend to be annoyed.

She said, "I forgot where I left my car."

"Fair enough," I said. "I've got news. They took Brandish in for questioning."

Amy smiled till her eyes twinkled. They were looking past me, seeing her retired dad living sane and free. She blinked tears, and they dropped down her cheeks. She caught the salty remains of one on the tip of her tongue.

"I knew we were going to win," she said. "So what do we do now?"

Amy was ready to finish him off.

"We wait."

We weren't even close to the homestretch yet, but I didn't want to discourage her.

"That's it? We wait?"

"We wait to hear from Brandish."

"You mean you want to hear from him?"

"Yes, I like to keep our relationship current," I said.

"Okay, so what do we do while we're waiting? Is there anything else you do around here?"

"What do you know about computers?"

"What do I need to know?"

"I need a lot of files backed up...all of them, actually."

"Great. Now I suppose you want me to clean up your computer chaos. But whatever. You're the boss. So are you going to trust me with your password?"

"Password? What password? Just make sure you don't take the games off."

I left her to it. On my way over to see Sally, the call came. He sounded hot and deserted, like congealed pea soup simmering on the stove all day. I was without sympathy.

I said, "I'm pleased they let you go so soon. I hope it wasn't too trying for you."

"I have been kind so far," Brandish said. "I know I need to make allowances for your strong will, but I am nearing the limit of my patience."

"There's nothing more I can do for you, so don't ask. My hands are tied."

"I do enjoy that image, but I'm not as much interested in your helping me as I am in helping you."

"There's nothing you can do for me. I'm set for life."

"That may be true the way you see things, but you are going to discover there will be a dispute over the authenticity of certain documents. In other words, there will be a need to determine where the truth lies regarding the church financial records. Do you see where there might be room for differing interpretations of events? Now if you were to see things my way, I am sure I would be able to prevent the authorities from prosecuting you."

"The only one who will be prosecuted is you. Get used to the idea. And if you need someone to threaten, why don't you make Braithwaite's life miserable? He's the one who thought up the scheme, isn't he, unless you're that stupid?"

"I am going to tell you again, Jane. There is more to our present situation than you can possibly know, and there are many prominent people in positions of power who have a vested interest in the outcome. The police merely went through the motions of asking me a few questions to satisfy certain people who want to make it appear that their sense of morality and duty are still intact, nothing more. Your friend Jillian is one of those, and Bert, of course, is inconsequential."

"If we lined you and Bert up, which one of you, do you think, would be identified as a human being?"

"I see. Well, you should soon be receiving a visit from the police yourself. There are a few questions I am sure they are eager to ask you."

"I'll look forward to it. I'm always happy to speak to the police."

"As you say, and don't worry about William. He won't be pressing any charges."

"That's sweet of William. Please thank him for me. I presume, in his line of work, he carries dental?"

"Don't concern yourself. He will be looked after. And as a point of interest, you might want to look at a feature in last weekend's *Globe and Mail*. It's a story you might enjoy about a church in Montreal."

"Thanks for the tip, but I've already seen it. Now, if you've had your jollies for today, I'll be signing off."

"There's more to come, dear. I promise you that. But you will get over it."

"You're becoming a bad habit." I hung up.

The downtown traffic continued its thick trail over the Lion's Gate and up the mountain. Nature was crawling with us. I'd seen the account earlier of the Montreal church fiasco. The story read like the church there was our clone, complete with the senior pastor as the alleged villain, a woman this time. The columnists were slapping happy about it there too. Here at home, the letters to the editor continued to jostle for position condemning Jessop's alleged malfeasance, and in New Jersey, a couple of rabbis were paying the piper for their part in a money laundering operation. The cry of the common folk was the same. Why did churches enjoy tax privileges while the rest of us bled red ink, when, as it turned out, there were men of the cloth, and women too, who were laundering money and fleecing the flock to stuff their earthly treasury? The odd letter pointed out that most pastors weren't, in fact, crooks, and far from being rich, a lot of them survived not too far above the poverty line.

Sally met me at the door. Her one-piece under her open terry cloth robe was wet. She'd been swimming. We went out to the pool, sat, and exchanged opening pleasantries, like I was the first to arrive at her exquisite party. A novel, *Paradise Loosed*, with a chick and a hunk on the cover, was open face-down on the patio table. I had to ask.

"So, you aren't able to go out of the house, but you don't mind swimming in the pool?"

"Oh, I went to the mall this morning to pick up a few things, and this is my first dip since I had it drained and cleaned. I'm improving steadily. Life goes on."

Sally looked like she'd lost a pound or two on her elliptical. Her bait was filling her suit just right. She wouldn't be swimming alone for long. But had she developed the discernment to screen out porn addicts, or was she on a course to reoffend?

"That's wonderful," I said, "that you are able to adapt so well after such a tragedy."

I'd tried my best to sound sincere.

"It wasn't that tragic."

She was sincere.

"Have you heard that Brandish was taken in for questioning?"

"Yes, Amy called me a little while ago to give me the news. Isn't it wonderful? I was so overjoyed I had to go for a splash."

Sally then waved her arms to simulate splashing, or maybe swimming. I wasn't sure which.

"I came over to tell you the news and to ask you if you have ever seen this man."

I showed her grinning William in happier times.

"Perhaps you might have seen him the morning Norman was killed?" I said.

"I don't think so. No, wait, he does look familiar somehow. But I couldn't be sure where I've seen him, that is, if I have seen him at all."

"Thanks, that helps."

"When this is all over, I'm taking a long trip, maybe around the world."

Sally was loaded for romance.

"Don't make reservations yet. It could drag on for years."

"What could drag on?"

"The Crown needs to determine who was responsible for what, charges need to be laid, court dates have to be set. It could take years, and don't forget the appeals."

"But what about Norman? I thought this was about him. Isn't he important?"

"I thought you were more concerned about your father now."

"I am, yes, I am. You're right, we should be more concerned about the living than the dead. The dead will take care of themselves."

I chose to skip a debate on her theology.

"Are you taking any medication?"

"Not much, only the usual. Why, don't I seem all right to you?"

"No, I just wondered. Not to worry, you are your normal self."

"Would you like some iced tea?"

She rattled the cubes in her empty glass at me.

"No, I only dropped by for a minute. I need to get back. I don't see why you shouldn't take your trip, if that's what you want to do. You don't have to wait till it's all over to do that."

"I would do just that, but the authorities have told me not to leave the country, at least not for now. I don't mind."

"Well, I hope you're able to keep yourself busy," I said. "Life can be hard at times."

Sally glanced at her novel, downed her iced tea dregs, and then stood to escort me out.

"Come for a swim sometime," she said. "It's fine well into October."

"That would be fun," I said.

On my return across the bridge, Amy called my cell. The police had been around to see me.

"What did you tell them?"

"I said you were training for a triathlon and I didn't know when you'd be back."

"What did you really say?"

"What could I say? You don't tell me what you're doing. And, by the way, what do you use this computer for? I can't find any case files, so what am I supposed to back up?"

"The files are in that locked cabinet to your right. Did you scan the thing and get everything updated that needs updating?"

"It's a lot faster now, if that's what you're asking."

"Thanks, I'll be there soon."

Amy sighed.

"I'm going for lunch," she said.

"Bon appétit."

I stopped by the police station. The detectives assigned to the case were glad to see me. I'd refused the offer of a dinner date from one of them a few months before. She didn't hold a grudge. They wanted to know simple details, like who was I working for when Norman was killed, and who was I working for the first time I delivered the church financial records, and who was I working for when I delivered them the second time, and who was I working for now? And didn't I think it was strange that I had delivered two completely different sets of books to the prosecutor's office in the space of a few days? I indicated that I was as dumbfounded as they were. Having looked into my history, they commended me for my cooperation in the past, both here and in Toronto, and commiserated with me over my father's passing. In general, they appreciated my coming in to see them of my own volition. The meeting was cordial. They instructed me to stay available for any questions they might have in the future. I assured them I was always eager to help law enforcement in the performance of their duty, knowing as I did the challenges such service entails. In closing, they applauded me for my commitment to good citizenship. Or that was how I intended to remember our time together. I was just as happy to be out of there. I needed a coffee and called Bert. He suggested lunch.

We met at a deli on Robson Street. The coffee and Bert's natural peace hugged my nerves until I stopped vibrating. I watched Bert eat.

"You knew they would want to talk to you," Bert said.

"Yes, but the boy and girl in blue were more intimidating than they had to be."

"Their noses are out of joint. When a crime is committed, they like to know about it first, not hear about it from our office. But there are other factors that influenced your interrogation, too."

"So, what are our chances?"

"Right now, slim and none. The high-priced legal talent is already coming out of the woodwork, and Brandish hasn't even been charged with anything yet. Plus, there are strings being pulled in the AG's office. There are some real heavy hitters involved in this. Jillian's just shaking her head. She knew it would be tough, but this is verging on the impossible. It's the evidence too. It could go either way. Your photocopies and audio aren't making a strong impression. The easier route is to hang Jessop and forget about tackling Brandish, and that's just the opinion circulating among the faithful, except, of course, for Jillian, who is not backing down. The powers that be, the ones behind tampering with the original documents, seem to be in control and aren't going to allow anyone to touch him. I'm sorry it's gone this way. We tried. As for your trip to the police station, you might take that experience as a personal warning rather than any attempt on their part to gain information."

I liked Bert's efficient summary, but I didn't like hearing it. We were stalled, Bert wasn't the fixer type, and there were no kind strangers around to stop and help us out.

"I don't like to be threatened," I said.

"You can't take them all on."

"But what if Brandish were to fall?"

Bert didn't answer, but his kind brown eyes loved me just the way I was.

"There's one other thing I would like you to know," he said. "It's not common knowledge, but when Pastor Jessop asked me for some legal advice a few years ago, he informed me in confidence that one of his girls was adopted. But you wouldn't know anything about that, would you?"

"If I did, it wouldn't be a subject I would want to dwell on right now. It would be unprofessional."

"And we wouldn't want that."

"No, we wouldn't. Not right now. Soon, maybe, but not right now."

Bert's kind eyes continued to love me, just the way I was.

"Are we on for tonight?" he said.

"No, I'd better stay home and recount my sins. I should be in a lighter mood by tomorrow."

The next morning at the office, I settled down to an hour of FreeCell and daydreaming about Bert. I'd put Amy in charge of sorting out my filing cabinet to stall her obsessive yanking on me for more information about Brandish and her dad. I'd thanked her earlier for speeding up my computer and told her I was confident she would do an excellent job with my files also. She recommended that I file my patronizing attitude under *B* or *S*, if I was able to find either of them. To underscore the pain of her filing trial, her repeated groan was, "I don't believe this," followed by a cute sigh.

After winning five straight, I said, "Bert wants to tie the knot."

"You're kidding. You hardly know each other," Amy said.

"We know each other well enough."

"He is a brave man. I suppose he's all about climbing your old bones on a permanent basis, and I mean that in a good way. Were you away sick when your teacher taught the alphabet to your kindergarten class?"

"I'm trying to come up with some good reason why we should wait," I said.

"How about the fact that most men are babies searching for their mothers?"

"Have you had a lot of bad experiences, or was it just one serious mistake that's made you so bitter?"

"Let's not get sidetracked," she said. "It's your love life we're talking about. Oh, isn't girl talk fun?"

"I think Bert and I are in love."

"Well, heavens above, the hard-nosed detective morphs into a budding tweeny. You're really serious, aren't you? It's hard to tell sometimes."

"Yes, I'm serious. I might just take a chance, and sooner rather than later."

"It's your life. And I hope it comes together better than these files. When is the last time you organized them? You don't pay me enough to do this."

"I might think about giving you a raise if and when you stop complaining."

She got lost in the files, and I lost myself again in FreeCell and Bert. Now that I'd rehearsed spilling some of my emotional life on Amy to hear how it sounded, I was about ready to dump the whole works on Bert. Marry Bert and get divorced from my justice mission. Let justice fend for herself. I wasn't obligated to be Jessop's savior. He already had a savior to share his life with. And now I had a life, too. Bert and I were a shoo-in for honeymoon heaven and bliss everlasting. But what about Amy?

"No, I really don't believe this," Amy said. "I don't know how you and your father stayed in business."

I took the call just before lunch. I listened to Jillian explain the details. She was thorough, and she was sad, and so sorry, but there was nothing to be done about it. But, she wanted to know, was there anything she could do for me? I told her there wasn't anything and thanked her for calling. After I hung up, I surveyed the familiar scene, the one I'd seen my whole life; it was a picture of the world and my place in it. And there I was, soon to be alone in my picture again. I consoled myself by remembering that everyone was alone. Life in this world was like that. You were alone. You came and went alone. God was supposed to be there with you, but I'd never felt Him, except that once. And even though that once was enough to know He was there, I still had good reason not to trust Him. Today was an excellent example of that. I especially never trusted Him with my dreams, because when I offered them to Him, I was always disappointed. My dreams were never approved of by head office, but always stamped *rejected* and sent back for upgrading. So, here I was again, on the verge of being alone. I knew that unless He was in favor of my dreams, they would never come true. Or were they supposed to come true? Either way, I'd given up following them, until Bert. But since God had never helped me with my dreams, there had been no chance for this one to come true, either. That was logical. My dad was logical. He said my childish dreams were nonsense. He didn't believe in dreams. He believed in himself, and getting the other guy before he got you. He said there was no God. I hoped for his sake he was right. Otherwise he had a lot to account for. But I knew he was wrong and accountable. And I knew there was a God, even though they found Bert's car down a cliff beside the Sea to Sky Highway. And Bert was in intensive care and was not expected to live. There were drugs in the car and the smell of alcohol, the police said. At first I thought they must have had the wrong Bert, but then I knew they'd found the one Brandish had created for them.

Amy asked me, why was I white, and, what was I staring at? I said I'd had a bad dream. She said she knew I hadn't had a bad dream because she saw me just now talking on the phone. I said it was a daydream.

"So then, who was on the phone?" she said.

"It was Jillian. She told me that Bert is in intensive care and he's not expected to live."

Amy gasped and dropped her file folder on the floor, the pages splashing everywhere. She came over to my chair and hugged my numb head. I felt like one of her family.

"What happened?"

"There was an accident…in his car. Brandish ran him off the road."

"Brandish? How do they know it was Brandish?"

"They don't. And no one is going to be able to prove that it was."

"I'm sorry," she said, and patted my head.

Then she remembered and said, "That ends our chances too, doesn't it?"

"No, we have one option left. I will wait for him to call, and then I will take care of it."

I unlocked my desk drawer. There it was, pushed to the back, my dad's snub-nose .38. I fondled it and then opened the box of shells. Amy stopped patting and let go of my head. She turned my chair toward her and clamped her hands on the arms. Her eyes screamed at me.

"Tell me you're not going to use that thing. Killing Brandish won't help us."

"It will help me. The devil doesn't have to win them all."

"He will if you play by his rules."

"It seems like they're the only rules in town."

"Revenge never solves anything," she said, and retreated to the other side of my desk. "If you go through with it, you can forget about me working here. I quit. But then what difference would it make to you? You will be in jail for life."

"No, not that long, probably only a reduced charge of manslaughter, and I'll be out in five for good behavior, but that doesn't matter to me."

"You are out of your mind. You should be rushing to the hospital to see Bert, not loading your gun."

"I've cried enough. Now Brandish is going to pay."

"Is it really only Brandish that you want to make pay, or is he only the scapegoat for your miserable life, and for your dad, and for everyone else who's hurt you?"

"Clever girl. You've got the picture. An all-inclusive, energy-efficient, one-shot retribution."

"I'm leaving. This isn't the kind of mentoring I signed on for, although I can't believe you are really going to do it. I hope by tomorrow you will be sane again. When you are, call me. I might reconsider my resignation. Right now you've got to go see Bert, if he's still alive. You might not get to see him again. No? You're not going to? Then you're a coward, or maybe you really are just out of your mind."

Amy gathered up her sorrow, anger, disappointment and left. I was just as happy.

I went home and refused to cry. No, I wasn't going to go and see Bert. I had no time for that. I wasn't going to go and watch him die. I was going to make myself useful instead. I was going to wait for Brandish, who, bless his heart, played the gentleman for the rest of the day. The waiting must have been hard on him. But as it turned out his book of etiquette did allow for the next day as sufficient time to wait. I was at the office when he called. I was thrilled to hear from him.

"You heard about poor Bert," he said. "I was shocked, but then I knew he had his challenges with certain substances, which, I believe, I did mention to you before. But who would have guessed he was capable of being so careless? However, there is one benefit to be had from such an unfortunate incident. Others will be discouraged from going down the same road as he did. You know what they say, every cloud has a silver lining, and speaking of silver linings, I was greatly relieved to hear he was alone at the time of the mishap and that you are safe and sound."

"Yes, I'm fine. I broke it off yesterday when I became aware that he had his problems, but I'm sad to hear this has happened. Do you know how he is?"

I replayed my voice. It sounded indifferent.

"It seems he is hanging on, but the prognosis, sadly, is grim. But I am pleased to hear you are coming to your senses and that we are beginning to see eye to eye. You sound like you might be ready to take advantage of my generous offer?"

"It depends on what you can do for me. I do admit I'm tired of being on the losing side."

"This is exciting. Why don't we get together and discuss future prospects? I am quite aware of your abilities, and I will assure you again, as I have in the past, that there is a prominent place for you in our organization."

"There's no harm in talking."

"That's fine. I knew you were an extremely intelligent woman the first time I saw you in church, the way your divine presence graced the pew. I am extremely gratified that you have come this far. I see no reason for us to delay any longer. I would be honored if you would agree to dine with me at my private club this evening."

"For a first date, I'd prefer a public place."

"As you wish, I am very easy to get along with. Do you have a preference?"

"I like Chinese."

"I know the best place for Chinese food in town, the Hong Kong Wok on Burrard. I'll send a car to pick you up at your town house at, shall we say, seven? I have some business to attend to, and then I will meet you there."

"I would prefer to drive myself. I would hate to inconvenience William."

"I see. Your point is well taken. That will be fine then. Make it seven thirty. I am looking forward to our time together."

"Yes, I expect it will be a night to remember."

"I heartily agree," he said.

I let him have the last word. He didn't have many left. His time on Earth was done. He'd been channeling evil long enough. Evil hated love and scorned the weak. To him love was useless except when it could be used as a weapon. And to him, Bert was now gone and forgotten, taken care of, and sentiment was absurd. Brandish was frothing to taste victory and was prodding me for some action. He needed to kill to survive. Predators were like that. They belonged in nature, but the human kind, like Brandish, were worse than animals. I hadn't talked to God about eliminating Brandish, but he hadn't brought up the subject to me either. I figured I was on my own. My heart wanted to break out and make its getaway down to the hospital, but justice and hatred barred the door. And besides, I didn't want the report of my grieving to get back to my dinner date. He might suspect I was fickle.

The Hong Kong Wok was an upscale Chinese food joint with white tablecloths and silver cutlery. It catered to those who perished the thought of eating urban-legend cat meat down in Chinatown. Brandish was already there when I arrived. I passed sweet William, who was idling at the door, and told him the temporaries looked sharp. Brandish was camped out at a corner table for two. It was going to be cramped. William came in and asked Brandish if I needed frisking. I told William I was resistant to that idea, and Brandish called him off. I was cold and focused. I pictured the splat dripping down the face of the gold-and-red dragon on the wall behind the fat head that now opened its mouth and spoke to me. But I looked real nice.

"I'm excited to see you," the head said. "And I am not embarrassed to say so."

I was embarrassed for him. He was heading south, and his lardy grin was about to sag when it drained. I set my black evening bag on the table at my right hand. He was too full of himself to notice. I felt nothing, no fear, no nerves, nothing. But I had to say something back to him.

"Our meeting on a social basis is long overdue."

"Exactly. And you do look extraordinary tonight. I can't help but think that it's for my benefit."

"I try to please."

"I have taken the liberty to order for us both, and lest you think such daring is chauvinistic of me, rest assured that imposing my will is not my intention. I have simply ordered all their evening entrées, and you can choose whatever you like from them. They are being prepared now."

He thought he appeared thoughtful and charming, but I suspected this was the way he ate every night, and his largesse wasn't intended for my enjoyment, but his. He'd also ordered a local Riesling ice wine. The server brought it and poured. I didn't begrudge him a final toast. The wine was good, but small talk was off the menu. I wanted his last words to count.

I said, "Since we're bosom buddies now, do you feel free to be more specific about the reason you brought the church down?"

Brandish laughed. The sound came from deep inside and rolled like a cranking engine. I hoped it wouldn't start.

"You aren't going to record my answer this time, are you?"

He laughed again.

"No, those days are over."

"I am glad to hear you see things my way. But you still have that curious need to know, to examine all the details, don't you? I like that. Such inquisitiveness can be useful in certain situations, if it is kept within controlled boundaries. But that is another subject."

Brandish sipped his wine and then became reflective, like he was about to bore the congregation with administrative details.

He said, "There are those in positions of authority who would like to see the church lose its preferential treatment concerning tax privileges. If tax-deductible charitable donations to churches were to be eliminated, there would be a sizeable increase in government revenue, not to mention the resulting income from the cessation of tax breaks on ownership of property."

"The public wouldn't go for that. There would be a revolt."

"You don't understand how public opinion works. The public doesn't have opinions unless they are orchestrated by those pulling the strings. You will be seeing more reports in the media of various church scandals across the country and then a greater public outcry for reform. But this is only to test the waters to discover the mood of the public and to see how well they can be manipulated. It will die down. The real purpose of the exercise will come later, and it's not really for us here in Canada anyway. We are small potatoes here. It's for south of the border. We are only conducting a trial run. Changes to Canada's tax law will follow later, as usual, after the Americans make their necessary amendments. You must understand that the economic challenges the Americans are going to face in the future will make removing tax breaks for churches seem like the necessary and natural course of events. And when the US tax code is amended to exclude tax breaks for churches and their donors, the increase in government revenue will be enormous. You will see that, over the next few years, even more scandalous and more numerous church breaches will be uncovered by our American friends, and the stage will be set. But it is nothing for you to be concerned about now, and it is certainly nothing that warrants any more of our attention this evening."

"Like I said, the public won't go for it. But what did Norman have to do with any of this?"

"Nothing. Nothing at all. Norman was greedy, a minor vice. And I was saddened by his passing, but, even so, the business our board was conducting had its best chance of succeeding with Jessop in charge. Norman was threatening that arrangement and was trying to find a way to get a larger portion of income for himself. I wouldn't be so tactless as to call his actions attempted blackmail, but I will say he thought he could use what he knew of our Whistler Village project as leverage. But Whistler Village is really a minor part of what we do. He didn't understand the scope of our organization. And then he died, at the hands of a party or parties unknown, which just happened to be to our advantage. So, you see, these kinds of fortuitous blessings need to be received gratefully when they occur. Take Bert, for instance. In his case, who could have predicted such an unfortunate turn of events? You know what they say, bye-bye Bertie."

He waited for me to acknowledge his joke, but I didn't think it was funny. When they buried his carcass in his piano case, he'd be playing a different tune. My gun was handy, but I hadn't finished my wine. I took another sip. I was stalling. His mention of Bert had found the combination inside me and opened the safe. I turned the clasp on my evening bag. Brandish furrowed his brow like he'd just thought of something. He reached for my hand but stopped when I pulled out a tissue and my compact. I dabbed, and he retreated. There she was in the mirror, my little-girl self. She was frowning and looking sick inside. She wasn't happy with life the way it was, the way things turned out for her, but that fact wasn't going to turn her into something she wasn't, and she wasn't a killer, and shooting Brandish was a waste of the rest of her life and of gunpowder. She began to cry.

"There is certainly no reason to cry over the demise of the church," he said. "Christianity has been dead for a long time. It only needs to be buried to get rid of the foul odor. Even so, the remains will be useful for a while yet. I am looking forward to moving on to my next church, once the postmortem has been completed on Pastor Jessop's flock. The congregation I have in mind is very large, and I have been informed by those in charge that they are in need of financial assistance and that my expertise will be sought immediately upon my signing up as a new member."

Through the teary blur, I noticed a man come in. He looked handsome in his black dinner jacket. His leather and jeans had been left in the closet. At our last meeting, he'd worn a brown bathrobe. But tonight he'd dressed to make an impression. His tattoos were hidden, except for the cobra peeking out from his throat. He came our way, sweet William behind him. I wiped my eyes clear to see Stan Sommers coming; he'd come to pay his respects. William nodded that Stan was unarmed, and Brandish smiled and extended his right hand for him to shake. Stan reached out his, but detoured instead, picked up a steak knife, and stabbed with it downward. Brandish received it once in the heart. His head jerked back and hit the red dragon's mouth, then forward it came to study its wine. Brandish's eyes could not believe it, but there it was. He stared at the last thing he would ever see. He fell sideways and wedged between the table and chair, his body unable to find rest on the floor. A blood blotch emerged on his white shirt, but his heart had stopped pumping, and there would be no more blood flowing. William pulled his gun and fired one round, just as Stan turned and slid the knife into William's chest. They fell united in a heap; the patrons were screaming. I stood and stepped back. Brandish's eyes were empty; William was dead and gone; Stan had met his Maker. It looked like I would be dining alone.

* * *

CHAPTER FIFTEEN

He had his tubes in all the right places and was sitting up when I got there. I could tell he was glad to see me.

"You're even sexy on your deathbed," I said, and kissed him on the forehead.

"I was beginning to think you didn't care," Bert said.

"I had some business to take care of."

"I heard."

Bert loved me with his eyes. I volleyed. Our understanding was renewed. I slid a chair under me and reached out to hold his hand. I felt like a wife and a mother. I could see why the roles were popular. They were an emotional blend a person might get used to.

"The specialist says they're going to put all your parts back together and you'll be ready to go back on the government payroll in a month or so."

"That's not all I'll be ready for."

"Have you forgotten you're not that kind of guy?"

"The accident…amnesia, I suppose."

I said, "I guess you know that Jillian is taking care of Brandish's drugs-and-alcohol frame-up."

"Not a pretty picture he tried to paint of me."

"No, it wouldn't have done you justice."

"Are you okay?" Bertrand said.

"I am now that I see you looking so bright-eyed and ready for action."

"You exaggerate, but thanks for the encouragement."

He closed his eyes for a minute, and I choked on the thought of losing him.

"We do have a future, don't we?" I said.

"I wouldn't have it any other way," Bertrand said. "And I've had a history of getting my own way."

"Not me. In fact, just the opposite. But I'm happy to take a ride on your success."

"I like the sound of that."

Bertrand's imagination drained him, and he dropped off to dreamland for about fifteen minutes, and I sat there holding his hand, my mind taking a rest too, like I didn't have a sad, complicated past but only a simple one of perhaps this morning baking his favorite cake and now hoping he would be home tonight to enjoy it with me. Then he opened his eyes again. He found some strength and gave my hand a squeeze. I remembered I wasn't Julia Child.

"Easy," I said, "you wouldn't want to get us thrown out of here, especially in your delicate condition."

He closed his eyes again and said, "I'm thankful." He paused and added, "I'm alive, and you're here. What more could I ask for?"

"Being vertical would be a good start."

He opened his eyes to stare me down.

"Don't act so tough," he said. "You don't fool me."

"I'd better go before I start singing *the sun will come out tomorrow*, and besides, they cautioned me about staying too long and raising your blood pressure."

I kissed him good-bye, this time in a more stirring way.

We parted, and he said, "I thought you weren't supposed to raise my blood pressure."

"Until tomorrow," I said.

I blew him a kiss and exited, humming nothing I recognized.

* * *

Back at the office, Amy pretended to work on the files, and I pretended to play FreeCell. She was happy I hadn't killed Brandish, but happy he was gone, but sad for Stan. Jillian told me Bert had helped Stan in the past with his legal troubles, all for free. We concluded that Stan decided not to let Brandish get away with it anymore, and with his previous experience in dirty work, he was a natural to do the job well.

Jessop had learned there were consequences to face for making compromises with evil. But there were also consequences to face for resisting evil. Brandish dedicated his life to enforcing that. The two of them had that much in common; they both had a working relationship with consequences. But Brandish had been privileged to receive further instruction. In a few seconds, he'd learned that evil doesn't play favorites, and then the lesson had ended. I skipped his funeral and Sunday's church service. Reports came back that his farewell gathering was smaller than expected. Stan's was scheduled for Tuesday. I planned to go. William's body was sent back to Chicago. I wouldn't be making the trip.

I lost the same game four times. It was time to quit.

I said, "I'm thinking about hanging up my magnifying glass. I can't see the point any longer."

"Has it occurred to you that you probably could use some rest?" Amy said. "I know you like to play tough, but this has been a severe trauma. And it's certainly not the time to make hasty decisions about the future, especially decisions that you might regret later."

"Thanks, Mother, for the advice," I said.

Amy's cell rang, and she answered. She listened for a few seconds and then said, "Slow down, Sally. Don't talk that way... You don't mean it...Okay...Just slow down...I'll be right over."

She flipped her phone closed and said, "It's Sally. She needs help. She doesn't know what she's saying. I think she's stepped over the edge."

"I'll drive," I said.

On the way there, Amy wore her seat belt and kept her feet on the floor. When she tried to talk, her mouth would open, her thoughts would jumble, and then she would bite her lip and turn and look out the window at the rain. I didn't push her.

I pulled into Sally's driveway and said, "I didn't really want to solve this case."

"I know," Amy said. "I didn't want you to solve it, either."

Jessop was at the door when we arrived. He was in his socks. Amy hugged him, took off her shoes, and we went into the living room.

"She will be down in a minute," he said. "She's getting her things."

We sat and waited for Sally. Jessop talked to the glass-and-brass coffee table.

"I'm not going to do them anymore," he said. "They can get someone else to do Alec's funeral and Stan's. I can't do it. I liked Alec at first, but then he changed. But then so did I. I liked Stan. I didn't like what he did, but I know why he did it. And poor Bert, he was the last one who should have paid. But there are consequences when corruption is allowed in the church. The innocent suffer."

He looked over at me.

"Ask Sally when she comes down," he said. "She knows there are consequences. She is not well, you know. I am responsible for that, but I am forgiven. Isn't that a remark-able thing? I am responsible, but I am forgiven. Others will suffer, and so will I, and I will pay the price in the end… when I get there."

Jessop was disintegrating again. His medication needed to be upped a few grains. But he had one thing right. Bert should have been the last one who paid. I'd think about my part in it later. The subject was too much for me to think about right now. We heard her coming. She hummed "Amazing Grace" as she came into the room. She wore brown suede boots and a light tan raincoat. She was going somewhere.

"Sit down, Sally, for God's sake," Amy said.

Amy was frightened.

"I have to go," Sally said. "I can't stay here any longer. There's a ghost in the pool." Then she shushed us and whispered, "I think it's Norman."

"They're coming to get her," Jessop said. "Do you think they might agree to take me instead?"

"No, I'm the one they want," Sally said. "Porn is one thing, but adultery is another. Although we all know that adultery is forgivable, if only he would have repented. But no, he wouldn't. He liked it. He was going to do it again… and again."

The doorbell rang. Jessop went to let them in.

"Can you believe it?" Sally continued. "He was going to leave me. He didn't think the church would care after my dad retired. He thought Brandish would save him and he would be senior pastor. Can you imagine? He was out of his mind. Sex mad. They would have thrown him out on his ear. And then where would we have been? Ruined, that's where."

Jessop led the two detectives in. We'd already met. One of them smiled at me.

"Her wet footprints were still in the hallway when I came home," Sally confided to us all.

"Don't say anything more," I said.

"They had been swimming naked," Sally said. "He was still out there, alone, not a care in the world. And the paddle was easy. What a surprise for Norman, but I would do it again."

Jessop slumped and resumed his communion with the coffee table. Amy sat, defeated, and began to cry.

"I'm ready," Sally said. "See you in church."

Then Amy jumped up and rushed over to hug and protect her sister. But Sally brushed her off and held out her hands to be cuffed by the detectives. Instead, the woman took her arm, and they led her out to the car.

"She's out of her mind," I said to Amy. "Don't worry. They won't go after her too hard. Jillian knows the history."

"Jillian, who is Jillian?" Jessop said. "Is she someone I should know?"

Amy went to console him. She sat and held his hand.

"No, it's all right, Dad," she said. "Sally will be okay. Her lawyer will take care of everything."

Father and daughter began to cry together.

"We should have gone with her," he said. "She's not well. But I'm not well either, am I?" He looked to Amy and then to me for confirmation.

"You will be fine," Amy said, "and so will Sally."

I hoped Amy's assurance was prophetic. Jessop and Sally were as sick as the institution they belonged to, the one that human ambition had created in its own image. The odds were good that Jesus was crying too.

* * *

CHAPTER SIXTEEN

I made an effort Tuesday morning to make it to book club, but I discovered when I arrived our group was going to be missing a few insights, permanently. Elsa said Lily and Winnie had turned in their reading lists. Lily told Elsa she was sad to leave, but her husband had decided to take his money elsewhere, and, as for Winnie, she was just too disillusioned for words.

"There was hardly anyone at church on Sunday," Anne said. "You can't blame Lily and Winnie."

"No one is blaming them," Elsa said, "and I will quite understand if you want to abandon ship also."

"I haven't had time to read the book," I said. "Things came up."

"So I understand," Elsa said. "I won't blame you for leaving either."

Since Elsa was making peace, I said, "You've done an excellent job of leading."

"I'm going to miss our time together," Anne said.

"Yes," I said, "I was starting to get used to your company."

"But we didn't become a family like the Joads," Anne said, "not even close."

"Maybe times aren't tough enough yet," I said.

"I, for one," Elsa said, "certainly don't want our economic challenges to get any more difficult, simply for the purpose of stimulating relationships."

Anne said, "I enjoyed *The Grapes of Wrath*. Who knows, maybe they will do a remake of the movie."

"There is no substitute for reading the book," Elsa said.

"There's SparkNotes," I said, "when you're in a hurry."

Elsa wasn't in the mood for me. She set her cup of green tea on the table, stuffed *The Grapes of Wrath* into her tote bag, stood, said good-bye to Anne, and exited.

"I suppose we are always going to be this way," Anne said, "at least on this side of heaven."

It was a neat summary. Then she said good-bye to me and sniffled out the door.

When I got back to the office, Amy was there. She'd skipped showing up on Monday again; her excuse was something about losing track of Labor Day. But at least this morning she'd broken her former crawling-out-of-bed speed record. She greeted me with the news that she'd do me a favor for now and continue the drudgery of being my devoted servant.

"But if a better offer comes along," she said, "I won't let any emotional attachment get in the way."

"What emotional attachment would that be?" I said. "I thought our relationship was shaky and might disintegrate at the whim of the film industry."

"You know the attachment I mean."

"Why don't you enlighten me?"

"How about the horrible fact that you *are* my mother?"

"How long have you known that?"

"I'm not stupid."

"No, you might even make a good detective one day."

"Is that the only way you can relate?" she said. "Everything's a case to you or a mystery to solve, and let's be detectives, and that will fix everything."

"Forgive me for being so shallow."

"There you are, going off again with the martyr thing," she said.

"Thank you for reminding me of my shortcomings. I'm looking forward to incredible growth in the future under your guidance."

"Oh, fine, have it your way," she said. "You are aware, I'm sure, that I told Adoption Services I didn't want any contact with you?"

"Yes, but I thought if you knew how sweet I was, you would have to change your mind."

"You know that there is a law against stalking?"

"I haven't been stalking you. I've just been getting to know you. And if you would pause to remember, you were the one who first contacted me, not the other way around."

"So then why did you move here from Toronto?"

"To see what I could see, and despite your imperfections, I like what I see."

"Well, I'm thrilled I pass inspection. But I haven't made up my mind about you. At some point we might even need to review the history of our relationship, don't you think, beginning at birth?"

"That's fair enough, since you are suddenly interested. But right now I'm still your employer. How about finishing the files?"

Amy faked her cute smile at me, turned with a flourish, and whipped open the middle cabinet drawer.

After a few minutes, she said, "No, I don't know how you stayed in business this long," and then to emphasize the drudgery of her task, she offered the folders another one of her cute little sighs.

It was hard for me to believe, but there she was, my daughter, willing to stick around. I wasn't alone. And even though my heart was on life support in intensive care with Bert, I planned to stay in business for Amy's sake. She was worth hanging on for.

Over the next few months, Brandish Corporation, with its head in the grave, began to decompose. Brandish had been the gunk holding the corporate corruption together. He'd made more than a few influential people unhappy during his corporate journey, and they became proactive in redistributing his wealth after his passing. His former drug-trade territory was snorted whole by the Asian connection, and the AG's office got into the act and decided to hang the church scandal on him posthumously. There was no respect for the dead. Mrs. Brandish was slated to suffer. Braithwaite disappeared, assets first, even before the word circulated that more heads were going to roll. There was a lock on the church door while the courts sorted through the financial debris, and a few hundred of the more rugged lost sheep were led away from the poisoned well by Pastor Gerard. They now assembled Sundays in a rented hall. The rest of the congregation had found pasture elsewhere, which contributed to cozier sanctuaries in the other Vancouver sheep-sheds. My daughter Amy became less difficult to get along with when she realized her dad was going to get an easy ride, and Sister Sally, who was being treated for her wayward mind, was touted at even odds to get away with murder. Amy and I eyed the French Riviera for a road trip to get our mother-and-daughter act together. Noble Bert, grinding through his physical therapy, gave us his blessing. I suspected that the dead detective in me would be resurrected by the time we got back. I'd lost a lot in life, and I'd found a lot. But since life was never perfect, I had to be just as happy.

* * *